The Listener

The Paranormal Investigator Series: Book 2

By

Christopher Carrolli

Christopher Carrolli

Published by
Melange Books, LLC
White Bear Lake, MN 55110
www.melange-books.com

The Listener, Copyright © 2012 by Christopher Carrolli

978-1-61235-503-0 Print

Cover Art by Caroline Andrus

The Listener
Christopher Carrolli

Found face down in a puddle of blood, Sidney Pratt is rushed to the hospital, where doctors diagnose cerebral hemorrhage as the culprit. Comatose, Sidney enters the realm of white light and takes a mysterious journey within it, where he questions his mortality. He meets the dead face to face and soon, the events of his life are played out, but his untold memory of a boy's voice unravels the team's next case…that of The Listener.

Photographer: Tara Manon

Christopher Carrolli is a full-time writer, who lives in Western Pennsylvania. He is a graduate of University of Pittsburgh at Greensburg and holds a BA in English Writing, and an AA in English. He has also won the Ida B. Wells Prize in Journalism. *The Listener* is Chris' second novel and second installment in The Paranormal Investigator Series. He is currently writing the third installment, *The Third Eye of Leah Leeds*.

www.facebook.com/ccarrolli
ccarrolli@facebook.com (fb email)
www.christophercarrolli.blogspot.com
carrollic@aol.com
www.goodreads.com/carrollic

And once again, this book is dedicated to my mother, Gladys Carrolli (1937-2011), and to my grandmothers, Della M. Carrolli (1915-1998), and Antonetta Emanuele (1901-1996).

And a special thank you to my sister, Micki Carrolli Beaver, and to my niece, Alexa Beaver for saving this novel, and to Nicholas Carrolli and Rhianna Beaver for their unending support.

Chapter One

It was a slight twinge of apprehension, a dark, fleeting fear she couldn't define that caused her to suddenly stir and stare ahead at the building. Sidney had been inside for far too long. Almost ten minutes had passed since he was to meet her in the parking lot. She'd left him in room 208, the paranormal investigative team's headquarters, where he was closing up shop, distressed and anguished over the death of Tracy Kimball. They were on their way to a somber, post-funeral gathering at Marcia Ross's house, and now they were late as Sidney lingered inside.

Leah Leeds slammed the door of the van with a sigh of exasperation. Sidney hadn't wanted to go to Marcia's; he couldn't face Tracy's parents, as he blamed himself for the tragic car accident that claimed her life. Leah became angered as she thought of his abounding ego that had displaced certain logic. She feared another explosion of heated words, picturing him basking in a flood of tears and sitting stubbornly motionless at the conference table. Either way, she had to go back inside to retrieve him.

It took five minutes to reach room 208. She pulled the heavy door slightly ajar and could hear the innate sound of rushing static coming from within. The tone of it sent chills through her, especially after the past three days of Hell that had enwrapped Tracy Kimball like a custom-made shawl. The monotony of the static's drone reached out into the hallway, but no other sounds could be heard.

"Sidney?" She called inside, pulling the heavy door wider.

"Sidney?" There was no response. She stepped inside, almost hearing the quickened beatings of her heart over the static. Her eyes caught the culprit producing the noise: the team's giant screen TV. But it hadn't been on when she'd left the room fifteen minutes ago.

Where was he?

She called out to him again, but this time, her voice stopped when her eyes met something on the floor behind the right side of the table. She stared in disbelief for what seemed like minutes, though it was only seconds. Sidney lay on the floor, face down, the blood smearing the side of his face and staining the carpet. She dropped her purse to the floor.

"Sidney!" She screamed out to him, her fleeting fear finally identified as he lingered near death in front of her. She fell to her knees beside him, touched his clammy skin, and checked his pulse. It was a slow one.

He's not dead. Oh God, not yet! Her thoughts moved fast.

"Sidney!" She screamed out again, and the pain in her voice brought the tears. Again, there was no response. She flipped open her cell and dialed 911.

* * * *

It was the second time within the past three days that Leah had witnessed an emergency response team arrive in record time to the aid of one of her friends. She prayed that this time was not too late. A crowd had gathered outside of 208 in response to her screaming; they stood peering, gawking, whispering, while Sidney, who was like a brother to her, lay deposed in uncertain trauma. She knelt beside him, and using a handkerchief from her purse, wiped away the blood that continued to trickle from his nose.

She heard the 911 responders shooing and parting the crowd. The throaty voice of a man called out—

"Step aside, please!" They set the gurney down as they neared. "Could you tell us what happened here?"

She explained that he was supposed to meet her outside; they were on their way to a post-funeral gathering.

"He was upset, and when he didn't come out to the parking lot after ten minutes, I came up here after him." Through breaking sobs, she described how she found him face down, the blood pooling beneath him.

"Was he in any kind of pain? Did he mention or complain of any sickness?" The EMT asked his questions with an urgency meant to prompt her mind into fast thinking. *Pain,* she thought, and then she remembered the headaches.

"I suspected he was having headaches," she said, and a wave of guilt washed over her as she remembered the twisting contortion of his face on one occasion. She told this to the main EMT, the man with the throaty voice.

"Are you his next of kin?" He asked.

"No, but we're close."

"Does he have family?"

"He's estranged from his parents. No brothers or sisters, just me." She felt a certain irritation at having to explain this.

"We'll need information," he said. "I'm going to need you to come along."

She was riding along whether he liked it or not, but thankfully, there was no need to assert this. Within seconds, they had Sidney strapped to the gurney with his head tilted upward and an oxygen mask tightened around his face. The crowd began to part once again, as the medics made their way through room 208 and into the hallway.

Many thoughts were bombarding her: What if Sidney died. She had to call Dylan over at Marcia's house. Would Sidney ever get to tell his side of the events that surrounded Tracy Kimball?

All of her thoughts and fears were suddenly silenced as she heard the EMT radio in to the hospital. The words he used cleared her mind like a vacated room.

"We have a possible cerebral hemorrhage." Fear stole her breath at the sound of it.

* * * *

She related all of the information she knew on the way, but feared it wasn't enough. She had no way of knowing if Sidney was allergic to anything, or if any pre-existing medical conditions were present in his family. He never spoke of his parents, only about how they failed to accept his abilities as a psychic being, which served as the rift of silence between them. His parents had feared his ability, eventually shunning the freakish manifestation that dwelled in their son.

Now as they burst through the doors of the emergency room, she realized it was time to call Dylan; he had to be here. The society most likely had Sidney's pertinent information on file, but Dylan, as chief investigator, would have to be the one to access it. They showed her to a small, outdoor area, where she would be able to use her cell phone, since cell usage was prohibited inside the hospital.

Dylan's phone rang four times.

"Come on, Dylan, pick up!" Her patience thinned.

Dylan finally answered on the fifth ring, and the sound of his "hello" was both quizzical and impatient. Like most people in a modern-tech world, he continued to use the most famous greeting even though she knew her picture had shown in his cell window. He didn't wait for her to speak.

"Where are you guys?" She could hear his irritation. "You were supposed to be—"

"I am at the hospital," she said. "Sidney's had a cerebral hemorrhage."

The silence of incomprehension lingered on the other end.

She went on to explain the rest: how she'd called 911 and ridden with the ambulance and now Sidney's information was needed. He needed to get to the hospital, now.

"We're on our way," he said, and the slightest hint of fear rose in his voice.

She flipped her cell closed and ran back inside just as the near lifeless Sidney was being wheeled by gurney into the triage unit. As she approached the fast moving team, a doctor she had not seen before reached out and stopped her.

"Did you arrive with him?"

"Yes," she said, trying to push forward. His hand gently pushed her back.

"I'm going to need you to stay out here."

"But—"

"We need you to let us do our job so we can assess the situation," he said, his voice calm to restrain her. "I will have questions for you, so please stay here." He was obviously aware that she would be supplying Sidney's medical information.

"I'll be here," she said, relenting.

The doctor turned away, steadfast and forward into the triage unit without saying another word to her.

* * * *

She hated hospitals, just being near one caused her stomach to have butterflies, and now she felt an entire swarm fluttering and dancing in a nervous flurry. Even the smell of hospitals was enough to unnerve her, that bleached, sterile cleanliness that lingered for hours in the nostrils. What was taking so long? She kept staring at the swinging double doors of the triage unit, waiting for the doctor to come back out and tell her that Sidney was dead.

What if they couldn't save him? What if they broke the news before Dylan and the others arrived? How would she tell them? A long, exasperated sigh escaped her as she let her clouded head fall between her knees. It had to be more than fifteen minutes since she'd called Dylan, around the same moment they'd taken Sidney inside. What had been mere minutes was in fact a torturous eternity.

The shock of the past three days was overwhelming her all at once. Today they had buried Tracy Kimball. Would they be burying Sidney, tomorrow, or the next day? This just didn't seem like it could be happening to someone like Sidney, so lively, active, a little overweight, maybe, but a young man. She should have done something when she saw how upset he was. The fast tragedy of Tracy's death had hit them all pretty hard, but it seemed to be so much more to Sidney; he'd adopted a personal responsibility toward her.

She breathed in and out, hoping the deep gasps of air would clear her jumbled mind. She lifted her head and looked around her—no sign of anyone yet. The constant buzzing of the overhead fluorescent lamps was maddening, yet the strong light being emitted seemed to be a watchful guard in the event of death; here, where death occurred often.

Then, out of nowhere, haunted memories of the Cedar Drive house flashed in her mind, all in vivid sequences. It had been happening a lot lately, especially in the recent days ever since she discussed her earliest trauma with Tracy. She saw Agnes' face for a fast, fleeting second. Agnes was the ghost that had watched over her as a child in that house, and now whenever she thought of her, other visions would follow: the moving rocking chair, the objects flying about, the woman Agnes' son had killed.

But the worst was the vision of her mother swinging from a noose tied from the towering height of the balcony. Leah hadn't seen this sight, but a manifestation of what it looked like would appear in her mind like a forbidden peep show. She winced, trying to shake off the momentary insanity that came along with it, tormenting her, trapping her like a mouse in a maze.

She was pardoned by the pulling sound of the automatic double doors of the ER and jumped from the chair at the sight of Dylan, Brett, and Susan Logan breezing through the electric entrance. Tears streamed down her face as she ran and embraced Dylan.

"Leah, tell me what happened." Susan's assertive tone was that of the quick, take-control doctor that they'd experienced only days before. Leah told the story again.

"Where did they take him?" Susan asked, her eyes searching.

She pointed in the direction of the triage unit.

"Wait here," Susan said, and brusquely pushed her way through the triage doors.

* * * *

In the same outdoor area where Leah had called him, Dylan pushed the number seven speed-dial button on his phone: the emergency number to reach Roman Hadley, the society's head director whom they had yet to lay eyes on. He pressed the speakerphone button, and both he and Leah briefed him on Sidney, requesting permission to access his file for the doctors. Strangely, Hadley expressed no surprise over what had happened to Sidney and had the information ready, as though he already knew. Dylan shrugged this off, thankful at learning that Sidney was not allergic to any medications, nor was there any known family history of disease.

Back inside, they spotted Susan, and the doctor Leah had spoken to, emerging from the triage unit. Leah hadn't had time to greet Brett, and now they sadly embraced, standing side by side. She quickly marveled how a sharpened Brett Taylor had looked with his hair pulled back into a slick ponytail, his mustache and beard trimmed neatly into a goatee, and the brown suede vest a noticeable contrast to the green army jacket that seemed almost sewn to him.

"Everyone, this is Dr. Talbot," Susan said, introducing the astute balding man with glasses. "I have explained to him that Sidney, being an only child, is momentarily absent of any next of kin given the estranged relationship with his parents, and that he works on campus with your society."

"Allow me to clarify, Dr. Logan," he said, holding up his hand before he would say anything else. "Did you say that Sidney is a patient of yours?"

Susan felt the urge to stretch the truth.

"He *was* my patient, Greg," she said reluctantly, calling him by his first name. "He ceased to be my patient when his parents stopped the sessions, but we have remained close. I was with him just today." They had not remained close, but this stretch of truth could not be proven otherwise. "I have known him since he was a boy, Greg, and I will take him on again as a patient if I need to."

He breathed heavily through his nostrils and looked at Dylan.

"And he works for you, right?" Dylan affirmed this and relayed the information in Sidney's personal file. "Then I will consider you both to be his next of kin."

"Just tell us what it looks like, Greg," Susan said.

"He's had a cerebral hemorrhage. We need to get him into surgery in order to stop the bleeding and relieve the pressure to the brain, and we need to do this fast. I need both of your signatures on the consent forms."

Brett held Leah closer as she released an audible sob. Susan and Dylan wasted no time in signing the papers.

"Will he be all right?" Brett asked.

"There is no way to tell at this point, but we're going to do the best we can."

"Please, Greg," Susan said, the sound of desperation in her voice.

"I'll be keeping you informed," he said to her.

He turned and made his way back to the triage unit and only seconds later, the gurney carrying Sidney was wheeled out, slower this time. With his head and neck set in a brace, and bandages wrapped around his head, he was stricken beyond pale, lifeless, not at all resembling the Sidney they knew and loved so much.

Leah continued sobbing and Susan made a steeple with her hands over her mouth as the fear, frustration, and worry stirred within her. They walked over to the gurney, being allowed a quick second to speak.

"Sidney," Leah's voice cracked, and she buried her face into Brett's suede vest. She couldn't look at him.

"I am here for you, Sidney," Susan said, calmly. "We are all here."

"You come back to us, Sid. We need you." Dylan's voice was firm, knowing that somewhere deep inside this shell was his friend, Sidney, who could hear everything. That's what he did best: he heard everything. He was a listener.

Their quick second at what could have been good-bye was over, and the gurney's pace became faster as it was wheeled into the waiting elevator.

Chapter Two

The voice, he could no longer hear the voice, and now the static seemed somehow faint, far-off. Above him, a brilliant sun gleamed yet it was not the bright orange face of Sol that was life itself, but a sun strangely steeped in the ultra-violet, and jagged were the arcs of the rounded orb. In front of him, a corridor unfolded, vacant and vast and cast in the purple hue that emanated from the strange sun.

The static grew fainter, becoming a hush in the hollow background where dark crude shadows danced in anonymity. Where was he? The long corridor stretched out even further with each small step that he took, becoming an endless plateau through which he moved, bathed in the dim, indigo light. His movement was hindered, weighted down, as though he moved underwater through a strange, uncertain sea.

He remembered the voice again—Tracy's voice. Then suddenly the images of the past few days played out before him, recreated on an eerie stage lit by the hovering sun. One by one, the images flashed like a slideshow: him tearing out of the parking lot with the van, Tracy's jeep flipping over the guardrail, her lifeless body bloodied as he cradled her, the sound of the ambulance, the casket, the funeral, the newspaper headline, the static—and then, the voice.

She's dead. Tracy's dead. Am I dead too? If not, why can't I wake up?

In the background where the shadows danced, he could see brief streaks of light that ran quickly away from the shadows. The images had stopped now, now that he recalled the last few events of his conscious mind. He remembered hearing another female voice, the one that kept crying out his name. He'd heard her only seconds ago.

Leah...yes...Leah. Was she crying because he was dead?

12

Another flash of memory depicted him hearing the voices during the desperate search for Tracy that began on the highway and soon ended on the rural back roads with another life lost to the infamous Shadow Valley Curve. It was the voices that had led him in that direction. One of the voices was his grandfather, the others were varied: men, women, older, younger. They were the voices of the dead that he'd heard all of his life, except for one—*one of them was alive!*

It was the boy. He knew he recognized the voice of the boy that night, but there was no time to think during the desperate race to save Tracy. He hadn't told the others about it afterward, but the boy he'd heard was alive, a living being, not a soul that had passed on as Sidney was used to hearing. Sidney listened to the dead, but this boy was alive, and he recognized the voice!

Memory: a boy of about ten, reddish hair, freckles, a much younger rendition of Sidney's ability. But this boy's ability, powerfully strong for his age, hears not only the dead, but the living.

The Listener...just like me, only...

The boy was one of the child psychics he'd studied in his research. His mother had brought him to the society for help.

Memory: A young woman, early thirties, strawberry-blond hair, big brown eyes, frightened by her son's ability. He saw her desperate frustration once again...

"I don't understand him. I don't understand it!"

He saw the boy at an older age...twelve? Obviously, Sidney had mentored the boy so why couldn't he remember his name. He had recalled the name that night during the chase, but now it was gone. He hadn't told the others, but it was the boy who found Tracy. It was Sidney who had been too late.

The images had passed quickly, and this strange state of conscious unconsciousness began to change, somehow altering itself from the slow motion void of which he had quickly become accustomed. The width of the vast corridor was shrinking, closing him in, trapping him in a state of motionlessness as now his legs would not move. He seemed somehow weightless, watching shapes float away, and the streaks of bright light that had intermingled now overpowered the fleeing shadows.

The indigo light grew pale in the presence of a blinding white luminescence. Was this the final exit? But, he wasn't finished. What about the boy? He had to tell them about the boy... He could hear voices, soft, but coming closer along with the light. Then suddenly the white light exploded, and the presence of another realm stretched out before him.

* * * *

The beaming hot-white of the overhead surgical lamp now illuminated the patient, showing the twisted face of his trauma with full and perfect disclosure. The side of his head had been shaved, revealing a light shade of purple to his scalp where the bleeding of the brain persisted. Dr. Greg Talbot's goal was to stop that persistence in hopes that Sidney Pratt would walk out of this hospital alive.

"Scalpel," Talbot instructed. The sharp silver gleam of the scalpel cut a glint before their eyes that constantly kept the surgical team aware of the instrument's power, a power to save and heal, but one false move could end and destroy.

A slight stream of blood surrounded the scalpel as Greg Talbot sliced into Sidney's scalp, his first strategic move to save his patient. Somewhere inside, on some uncertain level, Sidney experienced the brightness of the light, the pain of the incision, and a new realm of unconscious thoughts, memories, and dreams.

Talbot often wondered what transpired inside the comatose minds of his patients, especially this patient, one with a powerful psychic ability.

Chapter Three

Ryan threw the X-Box controller across his computer desk in frustration. What was the point in playing when the voices kept whispering what moves to make and ultimately beat the system? Besides, he was too worried about Sidney right now, and his mother wouldn't listen when he told her Sidney was in trouble.

When he saw the story on the news about Sidney's friend, the girl who went over the cliff, he tried to tell her then that he'd heard Sidney searching for her, and that the girl was in danger. She dismissed him. She didn't understand about the voices; she never did, and she never would.

Ryan had heard everything: the panic in all of their voices, Sidney screaming that they had to find her, the shouting back and forth as to which direction to drive. Shortly after, he'd heard that girl writhing in her own vomit. That's when he interceded, concentrating and channeling into Sidney's mind because one of the voices had whispered the words *"short cut."* Then came the sounds he would never forget: brakes screeching so loudly in his mind that the piercing sound caused him a slight headache, the repetitive crash of crushing metal and shattering glass, over and over again, and his beloved friend screaming out like he'd never heard anyone scream before.

"But, Ryan, how could you have heard Sidney?" she asked. "Sidney is alive, remember?" She had even called the university to ask Sidney Pratt to call. "You see, he is going to call when he can. He was not in the accident."

She did not understand, and he could not explain. He didn't just hear the dead. That's why he wanted Sidney, but Sidney was in danger. He was not in the car accident, but something else had happened, and Ryan could hear it all.

He could hear him moaning and writhing in pain, and something about Sidney's voice was different; it was somehow weaker. He wasn't sure how he knew, but it was Sidney's head, something was wrong inside his head.

It was two years ago when Sidney had explained it all to him that he was not limited to hearing the voices of the dead, but could also hear the living. Sidney failed to explain all of this to his mother because she refused to go any further in the study. She'd heard enough. She had learned to live with the fact that her son could hear the dead. It was more than she could handle, but she dealt with it. The end result was that Ryan would never fully understand his psychic capabilities; when she had ended the sessions, she had ended his right to understand.

Most often when he would attend his sessions with Sidney and the others at the university, his mother would leave for a while and come back to get him in a few hours. It gave them the chance to study him alone. The last time he was there the four investigators went into another room, an empty one next door to Room 208. They told him to relax and when they returned, he was to repeat anything that had popped into his "mental ear," during the time they were gone.

They closed the door behind them, and the room was silent except for the soft hum of the air conditioner. He stared around the room at all the equipment that fascinated him. The giant screen was huge so he failed to understand the point of all the other screens that hung from the walls, side by side. The various desktop PCs, the odd-looking machines, the gadgets and huge speakers, filled Ryan with a curiosity that sparked a thousand questions.

Suddenly words formed, and voices spoke inside his mind like a far-off radio. Sidney had explained that the rooms were soundproof and what that meant. There was no one in the room, but Ryan's young, sage green eyes searched around anyway—he was alone. They'd told him not to resist the voices, and this time he didn't; he'd recognized them clearly...

* * * *

"Well, guys, he's what's called a clairaudient," Sidney said in Room 209.

"Which means what, exactly?" Dylan had wanted Sidney's expert opinion. After all, it was his area of expertise.

"It means he is an extremely powerful listener, probably even more capable than I. This kid doesn't just hear the dead, he hears the living as well."

"He's capable of remote hearing?" Leah asked the question with a gasp of astonishment, and they all felt the slight ripple of shock at the newest discovery. Sidney nodded his head.

"And that's what we're testing, right now, I take it?" It was Brett's voice.

"Yes," Sidney said. "Leah, come up with a password."

"A password?" she asked.

"Yes, you know a word that tells us whether he passed or failed."

Leah rolled her eyes upward in thought.

"Listener," she said, picking the obvious.

"Great, let's go back inside."

The investigators walked back to Room 208, entered calmly, and sat down at the table with their young guest. They knew their eyes beheld a prodigy, but to what extent was uncertain. Since he was a listener, it would be Sidney who would have to determine that.

They had empathized with Ryan, as well as the plight of his young mother who left him here. Being endowed with a powerful psychic ability at such an early age was in many ways a curse. No one knew this better than Sidney and Leah.

"So, Ryan, I'm sure you know what we just did, right?" Sidney got right to the point, and Ryan nodded his head.

"Then, Ryan, what is the password?" Sidney asked the question as the four sat waiting, pulses racing, yet knowing.

Ryan looked at the four anxious faces in front of him and answered. "Listener..."

Their eyes grew wide, and focused on each other.

* * * *

That was two years ago when he was ten. Now that he was twelve, the voices came more frequently, and he could tell who was dead and who was alive. It was a difference in sound. One sound was abrupt, out of nowhere; the other had always been there, though unspoken before. Then sometimes the dead spoke all at once, overwhelming him with overlapping words to the point where he wanted to scream, but couldn't. Sidney understood; Sidney could help him control it.

That's why he had to get to him; they could help each other. Ryan could hear Sidney's voice; it sounded as though he were trapped, lost somewhere and unsure how to come back. He also heard the voices of the others, Sidney's friends. The blond girl, Leah, she kept pleading for Sidney to come back, but where had he gone?

Yet there was another voice that Ryan didn't understand, and that's why he had to move fast to find Sidney and the others. The man, the man was alive, speaking on the phone. He'd heard bits and pieces.

"Sidney Pratt...no longer an option...there is another...the boy...we've got to find him...I'm telling you, I heard him myself!"

Every sense of knowing that stirred inside him told Ryan that the man was talking about him. The man, he was a listener too, and he was listening now. Ryan heard the man's name spoken—Hadley. He wasn't a good man; he was a bad man, and the others didn't know everything about him. If he was right, the man was coming for him. He had to get to Sidney and the others fast.

His first instinct was to catch a bus to the university, but they weren't there. Ryan had figured that out when he'd listened with his mental ear as Leah cried for Sidney to come back, and in that distant background he'd heard a voice on an intercom, like in a hospital...

"Dr. Talbot to the ER, STAT...Dr. Talbot to the ER, STAT..."

The hospital, Sidney was in the hospital. He may not have been in the accident, but he was there because of his head. Ryan knew it; he could hear it. Sidney had to be at University Hospital, which was a fifteen-minute walk from Ryan's house. He could make it, but he had to slip down the stairs and through the front door without his mother seeing him. Even if she didn't, she would notice that he was gone within an hour. It didn't matter. He had to find the investigators and fast. His mother just wouldn't understand.

Step by step he silently crept down the staircase of the modest two-story, three-bedroom house. His tiptoes arched down on the carpet barely made a sound. He spotted his mother from behind in the kitchen. Thankfully, she'd left the front door open; it was a cool, late afternoon in October. The clamor she made in the kitchen covered the sound of the creaking screen door as he slipped out into the dusk.

* * * *

Annie Quinn stood at the stove making fried chicken; it was her son's favorite. She had been doing everything lately to be more encompassed in his life: making his favorite meals, going to the movies, doing things together, anything to keep his mind off Sidney Pratt and those paranormal investigators.

It was difficult enough having to endure her son's unexplainable psychic abilities, but to have him studied under a microscope and watching them hone his "gift" to become the main focus of his life was definitely not what she had wanted. She wanted her son to go to school, play soccer, play video games, get married one day, but for now, she just wanted him to be a normal kid. She would never forget what Sidney Pratt had said to her...

"But, Annie, Ryan is *not* a normal kid."

That's when she stopped the sessions altogether. She thought of all this as she flipped the browning chicken in the pan, her long, strawberry-blond hair pulled back into a ponytail. It was difficult, having to explain in detail the first instance in which Ryan had displayed this strange ability. She hated rehashing what had happened that night; she still wasn't even sure she believed it. She had chalked the whole thing up to some strange coincidence, an eerie déjà vu that occurs in times of trauma, just something that happens...

"What coincidence 'just happened'?" It had been the blond girl, Leah, who had asked that question with just the slightest hint of what was either intolerance, or disapproval. She paid it no mind as she reluctantly explained.

"Ryan's father was murdered," she said, and a dead silence had descended upon the room. Thankfully, Ryan had not been with her for that session. The four investigators had asked to see her alone, and now they waited for her to continue.

"The night it happened, Ryan woke up screaming for his father. Ian, Ryan's father, was not home yet; he was out." She looked over at them, hoping to convey the meaning of her last few words. She and Ian were married not so much out of love, but because she got pregnant, and many nights he'd left her and their son alone while he stayed out partying, boozing, carousing. They had stayed together in a broken marriage for Ryan's sake.

"I ran into his room, and he was awake in bed screaming. He grabbed a hold of me and pleaded with me that his father had been shot; he'd heard it. I tried desperately to convince him that he had been dreaming, that it was nothing more than a nightmare, but he was unyielding. He kept repeating that he'd heard his father arguing with someone, and soon after, he'd heard a gunshot; then, he said Ian was calling him.

"This was the first time. He managed to fall back to sleep, after I had convinced him that his father was still out, working overtime, and that he would be home soon.

"'But Mom, I heard him!'"

"He said this to me with this certainty, this conviction that I had never seen before. It rattled me inside. I laid on the living room couch, unable to fall asleep the rest of the night, and it was about four in the morning when there was a knock at the front door. As I neared the door, my heart was both pounding and stopping. What Ryan had said was echoing through my mind.

"It was two police officers, coming to tell me that Ian had been shot in the alley behind Marty's Tavern. There had been a dispute over drugs, and from what they had gathered, Ian had been at the forefront of the episode. Obviously, they didn't have the whole story yet, but I could think of nothing else but whatever it was that stirred Ryan from his sleep only hours before, causing him to launch into the tirade that he did. I was speechless, frozen, and I recall the officers taking me by the shoulders and sitting me back down on the couch.

"What in God's name was I supposed to tell my son when he woke in the morning, that his nightmare was real, but not to worry, Daddy had gone to heaven? Nothing was real to me anymore at that point. They started asking me questions. Was I aware of the extent of Ian's habits? Whom he was dealing with? I wasn't listening; it was as if I couldn't hear them. I kept hearing Ryan's outburst earlier and kept touching everything around me to make sure it was real. It didn't seem real, but it was.

"They assumed that my state of shock was a result of Ian's death, but if they only knew. They decided to come back later at a more appropriate time when I could answer questions. They knew I had to wake my son and tell him, a task for which I was completely unprepared.

"When he woke, I did the hardest thing I had ever done in my life. From then on, my son talked of hearing voices, some he says are dead, and sometimes he hears neighbors, people at the other end of the phone before they call, and other things I can't explain. He still hears Ian from time to time, and when he does it drives me crazy."

No one broke the silence, and an eternity passed in only seconds.

"Look, I'm not even sure I believe this, okay," she said, frustrated.

"I don't know what else to do. I mean, how can my son be crazy? He predicted his father's death as it happened. I don't know what to make of it all. I wasn't raised to believe in any of this, and I don't know how my son became the way he is, but I know one thing, he didn't get it from me!"

What she had said was not the entire truth, and she'd kept her head down, her eyes averted. Then, it was Leah Leeds who asked the next question.

"Annie," she said, and at that moment, Annie felt the brusque tension between them.

"Were you also involved in Ian's drug activity?"

She noticed the other investigators look at each other, surprised and perturbed by their colleague's interjection.

"No," she said, curtly. "I was not."

Then why did you stay with him, knowing that you had a child to protect?

This thought went through her own mind; she could only imagine how quickly it went through that of her detractor's.

Sidney Pratt had interrupted the tension, explaining to her that her son was a clairaudient or what was called in earlier times, a "listener." Other modern terms included words like "channeler," and "medium," but the term referred to one who possessed the psychic ability to hear those who had passed on, as he put it. Sidney was cursed, in her opinion, with this ability as well. He'd summarized his life story for her, not that it helped, in fact, it scared her even more for her son's fate.

They had asked about other instances after his father's death. She was reluctant to describe them. Raised in a strong, religious family, she was taught that even discussing this type of thing was a taboo. And what if after she told them, they carted Ryan off to who knows where? She didn't know these people.

She would soon relent, telling them about Ryan's knowledge of one of her high school friends, who had died in a boating accident while vacationing in Florida. Ryan would have had no way of knowing any of it. There was also the elderly neighbor across the street; the one Ryan claimed would die soon because his late wife was coming for him. The man was dead three days later.

None of them was surprised.

"So, Annie, if you're not a total believer in psychic abilities, why did you seek us out?" It was Dylan, the leader of the team, who had asked.

"Because they have a name for people who hear voices," she said, emphasizing, her voice rising. "My son is not crazy!"

"Then you came to the right place," Brett said. "We can help Ryan."

They had agreed to a number of sessions with Ryan alone and several with both of them together. She gave her consent and signed all the papers, but the sessions went unfinished. They were teaching Ryan how to use and to live with this "ability." That was not what she had in mind; she was hoping that they would help him to suppress it.

"But, Annie, Ryan is not a normal kid." She would not let her son be a Guinea pig.

She insisted that Ryan dissuade himself from acknowledging this ability, and try to live a normal life. At some point, he realized just how scared she really was, so he complied. That's how they had lived for the past two years, with no mention of it, until the past week when a young woman, a friend of Sidney Pratt's, was killed in an accident. The headlines were everywhere. Ryan swore he'd heard the whole thing, and that Sidney was somehow in danger afterward.

The naked past she'd tried to clothe was stripped bare again.

In some strange way, she could understand the reaction the Leeds girl had toward her. Subconsciously, she was putting herself before her son, and Leah had picked up on it. She went there asking for their help and at the same time, expressed her disbelief, her irritation, and worst of all, her fear. She didn't blame her, but that's what they didn't understand...her fear, and why.

The smell of the searing chicken roused her out of the reminiscence. She noticed her dark brown eyes in the translucent glass of the microwave-range, yet another trait Ryan had not picked up from her. He somehow got his Dad's eyes, those sage green eyes that somehow dominated over hers. But that's not all that Ryan had inherited from his father, and from that fact, fear had spoken loudly.

* * * *

"Ryan!" She called out to him as she normally did when dinner was ready. There was no answer. She called out again as she walked into the living room, then glanced out the front door, seeing he was not on the front porch.

He was not in his bedroom when she went upstairs to check. She ran back downstairs and called out to an empty basement.

"Ryan!" Still no answer met hers, and the vacant, lifeless, sound of being alone assaulted her ears. He wouldn't go to a friend's house without telling her, so she called his cell phone—no Ryan. It went straight to voicemail. What began as concern turned to panic and soon gave way to anger. She knew full and well where he'd gone. He'd begged her to take him to the hospital to see Sidney when he didn't even know that he was there.

No doubt, he'd walked to the hospital. The inevitable had finally confronted her; she had wondered how long it would take. Her face was fuming a soft red as she snatched her car keys from the kitchen counter.

* * * *

The walk to the hospital was longer than he anticipated. He had been walking at least fifteen minutes, and even with the hospital's heliport in plain view, he still had another five minutes to go. He realized that he should have waited until after dinner to leave, but darkness came early this time of year, and that would have been too late. Mom was cooking, and when she was done, she would notice him gone. He had turned his cell off, but he would hear her wrath one way or another.

She will be furious about me sneaking out of the house and leaving without telling her, but once she sees Sidney in the hospital, she'll realize that I was telling the truth and not imagining the whole thing. She would also rave about the distance and walking alone, but he knew how to disarm her. He enjoyed walking; it cleared his head and often made the voices disappear for a while.

Either way, he had to get to Sidney and the team to tell them about this Hadley guy. If Ryan was right, he was coming for him. In his mind, he kept replaying the ominous phone call that he'd "overhead." He knew the team would believe him, especially after they heard the whole story.

As he neared the hospital, he was thankful to have a few minutes to himself just walking, letting the voices subside, and allowing his head to clear enough that he could think. He'd been thinking about his father lately, but then again, he always thought about him. The night his father died would be the one event in Ryan's life that he would never forget as long as he lived, and he would never forget his voice.

He had been shaken from sleep by the sound of that voice.

"Ryan!" He'd called out in desperation. He'd heard the fear in his father's voice, real and almost childlike. His father, tall, strong, burly,

was not afraid of anything. *Nothing would ever scare Dad*, Ryan had thought. But the unmistakable sounds of fright and panic in Dad's voice had shaken that faith and scared all reason from him. *Why did he call out to me that night?* He thought, and then guessed he'd never know.

Then, there was the sound of the gunshot. He knew it was a gunshot because it was just like on TV: loud, hollow, and echoing. When he told his mother, she called it a nightmare. He'd had many nightmares before, but none that involved his parents. But, somehow he knew, deep down inside of him, that his Dad was dead. When his mother told him the next day that the nightmare was real, that's when the voices began. Soon after, he'd met Sidney and the gang.

Now he had to get to them, and he could hear the hospital's automatic front doors opening and closing as visitors entered only feet away. He had made it, feeling a sense of relief as the automatic doors opened for him. He would inquire at the front desk and ask about Sidney Pratt.

Chapter Four

Roman Hadley was comfortably situated in the leather armchair behind his long mahogany desk cluttered with files, papers, and other debris. The phone call he'd just finished reverberated through his mind.

"Obviously, Sidney Pratt is no longer an option," he'd said to the voice on the other end. "What kind of situation Sidney will be facing when he wakes, if he does, is anyone's guess? He may no longer retain his psychic abilities, or it could be even worse.

"But there is another option. About two years ago, Sidney studied the case of a young boy, who was immediately pronounced as clairaudient. This boy, Ryan Quinn, was discovered by the team to be strongly enabled of 'remote hearing.' He picked up an entire conversation in another room—verbatim. I read about it in the brief file they'd kept on him. Soon after, his mother halted the sessions.

"I'm telling you, this kid is a powerful listener with an ability that's a little more substantial than Sidney Pratt's. Unlike Sidney, he is not limited to hearing the dead. Ryan can hear the dead *and the living*. Where Sidney hears words, sounds, ghost voices, Ryan hears sentences and live conversations. In his life, Sidney has only caught brief spoken words of living voices. Though he may not know it yet, Ryan was one of those voices; he called out to Sidney during the search for the Kimball girl."

"Is it possible that the child is also some form of developed telepath?" The voice on the other end was a calm, collected, monotone flow evoking strategy.

"Yes. He is still a child, which means his psychic abilities remain at their peak. We have got to find him! He could be the key to unlocking the power behind this project. I'm telling you, I heard him myself!"

The last emphatic statement that Roman Hadley nearly shouted needed no explanation to the voice on the other end as he slammed his private cell shut. He himself had once been a tremendously gifted clairaudient, possessing the ability of remote hearing since childhood. But now, at the age of sixty, time had eroded and erased the strange capability down to a random minimum, a fact he had never understood. He remained enabled enough to keep tabs on his closely watched team of investigators, especially Sidney Pratt, and the thoughts and sounds of Ryan Quinn were as clear as a ringing bell.

Though his clairaudient ear was fading, his telepathic mind remained strong. But the project needed fresh blood, a younger, newer listener, one at a psychic peak; a powerfully gifted listener like Ryan could be developed into a psychic genius. From his private, clandestine office, he glanced at his aged reflection in the immaculate picture window that overlooked the famous steel city.

The wisps of gray that streaked his black hair had turned it to a shade of salt and pepper, and his eyes now seemed a faded blue, as time had also eroded the prominent features that had once made him handsome. His rough, rugged, countenance stared helplessly back, a time-beaten and withered contrast from the young soldier once called into action to fight a war his friends were deeming wrong, unjust...

The height of Vietnam and the tumult of 1969 had been everywhere. War was ongoing, coffins came home endlessly, many of which belonged to friends he'd grown up with since childhood. Drugs, sex, freedom, the feminist movement, the counter-culture, the riots, all of it still flashed through his mind. All of it was a chapter told long ago, a life once lived, but not forgotten.

It was his eighteenth birthday when his number matched one of many drawn in the draft call. He would never forget the look on her face when the civil service announcer called his number exactly as it was printed on the card; she looked like the world had ended for her. He remembered the way his heart sank deep into his chest, and his legs quivered as all their plans were cancelled by the fast drawing hand of fate.

"We'll go to Canada," she'd said, grabbing onto his shirtsleeve, but he knew that would be pointless. Living a life of refuge for an indefinite period of time, even after the war was over, taking her away from her plans, her dreams, her career, her family, was not what he'd wanted for her. Besides, it wouldn't be that long; Nixon was about to end this debacle...soon. Where Johnson had failed, Nixon would succeed, and everyone would be coming home. He would be back, and they would start all over, at least that's what he'd thought.

He'd been deployed to the South of Vietnam where fierce, mortal firefights bloodied the deep green of the Mangrove jungles. The Mekong Delta still lived in his mind with the finest of sharpened recollection: the endless green, the vast land populated with thatched-roof straw huts from which peeping heads peered out in fear and curiosity, the daily explosions, the sneak attacks, the gunfire, the blood, the cries.

There was the time he'd been helping to repair a bridge of its sections that had begun to fall away, when the deafness overcame him. It could have been a side effect of the battle sounds to his hearing, but lately he couldn't tell. He glanced around him as voices that didn't belong began to speak. Young male voices spoke in their native Vietnamese, which he didn't understand, but he did recognize the word for attack—*tan cong*.

"Sergeant!" He turned and yelled directly to his task-sergeant superior. *"Incoming! Incoming—they're about to attack us!"*

The puzzled look on the sergeant's face prompted the surge of panic that snapped inside of him. He didn't understand; none of them understood about the voices he'd lived with his entire life. He'd never mentioned his psychic abilities to any of them, especially when they'd interviewed him. It was something he never discussed; he was brought up to believe that taboo was not to be mentioned, and exploration was out of the question.

"Sergeant, they're about to attack us from the west side—I heard it! You don't understand—I heard it!"

The look on the young sergeant's face turned to curiosity, almost accepting of the assertion, but it was too late. The sounds of explosion and gunfire had erupted everywhere. The bridge had imploded, crumbling under a burst of orange flames that suddenly swallowed it. Around him, his fellow troops twisted and twined, battered and beaten by the barrages of gunfire that riddled their bodies. Many had hit the ground in time, firing back at unseen enemies safely hidden by the surrounding foliage.

His task-sergeant had grabbed him by the shoulders, and in an instant, threw the both of their bodies over the side of a small hill near the bridge. Once they took cover, the sergeant began radioing then drew fire on the invisible attackers. The battle lasted almost eight minutes, and he could still taste the sulfur of smoke and ammunition as it had choked and blinded him that day. Seven of his fellow troops were killed, fifteen were wounded.

Late that night, he was awakened from his bunker and told not to make a sound. Two soldiers waited while he dressed and stood at attention, groggy and mystified.

"You're wanted. We've been told to escort you."

What was happening? Was he being sent home? Did they think he was responsible for what had occurred? He knew he hadn't done anything wrong. He only tried to warn them, but how was he going to explain knowing?

As soon as they were outside of the barracks, one soldier held him in place, the other blindfolded him, wrapping and tying the fold tightly just above his ears. The fear was yet another explosion, though this one inside of him. Once his heart began beating again, it pounded, and breathing became harder as his lungs quivered in his chest.

"Just a precaution, that's all." The soldier who tied the blindfold, not much older than he was, tried to reassure him.

"So, obviously, I'm not going to headquarters..."

The soldiers didn't answer him.

Now the vibes of fear churned, causing a shudder through his body. The sweat poured down his face, nearly soaking the blindfold. He could feel some dark, ominous force about to change his life forever, and he was right.

* * * *

The first thing he was able to recognize was the downward drop of an elevator, and when it opened, feeling the coolness of the air around him, a quick change from the July heat. *Underground,* he thought. He focused and tried to listen with his ability, yet could hear nothing. His ability seemed to evade him in times when he could have used it.

He heard the elevator doors close behind him with a heavy clank and could see increasing light as each layer of the blindfold was unraveled. The light was a dim, dingy basement glow that cast shadows upon the dank and darkened walls.

"This way," the soldier said, turning him to the left. He was instructed to walk in front of them down a long, underground corridor.

All around him, he could see doors that contained security light panels. He tried to listen beyond each door, but dead stillness had greeted his mental ear, as though nothing dwelled in this vast sub-terrain except the silence of well-kept secrets and the muted past of histories long fulfilled.

"This one." The soldier's words were few and limited as he motioned him to a door on the right-hand side of the corridor. "You're expected. Just press the red button to enter."

As soon as his finger pushed the bright, glowing red button, the door to the room drew back sideways in an electric hiss that seemed almost futuristic. Strange. He entered the small room that housed a metal table with three metal chairs, two on one side, and one on the other. A large, opaque, glass window stretched across the back wall, cloaking and hiding what or whoever watched beyond it, another ominous feeling he couldn't ignore.

A man in his late forties with dark hair slicked back sat at the small interrogation table. He had never seen him before; he didn't even look military, but something was top-notch about him. He looked up from the file he was reading and spoke.

"Welcome, Private. Please, have a seat."

The man's voice was calm, inviting, and friendly, and invitation to be at ease.

"I am Agent Foster; FBI." His young eyes grew wide at the mention, but the man made a dismissive motion with a shake of his head and the quick close of his eyes. "We understand that you were part of the unit that was hit by the sneak attack today?"

He nodded his head.

"It has also come to our attention that you predicted the whole thing only seconds before it happened." He noticed Foster's eyes brighten in fascination as he stated the fact in the form of a question.

Suddenly afraid, he cast his eyes down at the table. He felt cornered, clueless as to what his response should be. For the first time, he was confronted with something he never talked about and was free not to. He'd been so safe at home, where the ability would never come to light. Now it was exposed, and he felt the immense strain of an imagined witch trial. He looked up again at Foster, speechless.

"You reported to your task sergeant that you 'heard it.' Is that true?"

He didn't respond.

"There were witnesses, at least five of them so far."

The elder agent sat with his fingers pressed together in a steeple, while the young soldier pursed his lips together, safer in silent sanctuary. The agent watched and recognized this, then spoke for him.

"Let me tell you what I think, Private. I think you possess a very rare psychic ability that you've most likely endured all of your life. This unique talent, as I see it, is known as 'remote hearing,' something that your background has taught you to repress. You're afraid to talk about it because you fear retribution, or that you have done something wrong. Am I right?"

The young soldier's lips parted then closed.

"Only moments ago you scanned this underground with your ability and failed to hear anything. Do you know why that was?"

His heart pounded harder as the agent stupefied him, but still he did not respond.

"I know all of this, Private, because I am a clairaudient myself."

Surprise and relief washed over him. He felt his breathing stabilize. It was the first time he had ever heard the term before. He had heard others like listener, channeler, but the scientific term told him that Agent Foster knew more than he did.

"I could hear the soldiers speaking to you, and your thoughts as you tried to listen, as we call it. Our ability is a form of telepathy so I was also able to hear words that formed your thoughts. I remained quiet and cloaked my own thoughts to test the extent of your ability."

"Did I pass?" He spoke finally, unsure of what to say first.

"Most assuredly, now let me explain to you why you're here. What I am about to tell you, Private, is top-secret, classified information, of which I have been given clearance to divulge to you. When I finish, you will then be subject to the FBI and its involvement as it pertains to you. I will then brief you on what will be the next course of action, as far as your deployment is concerned. Do you understand?"

He was slightly afraid again, but he nodded his head.

Agent Foster then briefed him on the Bureau's budding project that involved the study of remote viewing. He described human subjects equipped with the ability of seeing people, places, and objects in remote areas simultaneously, and how they were being studied and utilized in areas of national defense.

"The powers that be, however, are beginning to shun the results of our efforts even though great progress is being made. In those efforts, we have discovered subjects that we have only recently encountered—clairaudient listeners, such as you, people who are enabled of the opposite psychic ability called remote hearing."

He wondered how collectively Agent Foster was using the word "we." Though he didn't fear him, something about the elder agent struck him as an outsider, a vigilante.

"Our studies in this area of psychic ability are, in fact, continuing at this moment. How beneficial the employment of such abilities will be toward our nation's defense in the long run, we are incapable of knowing. That's why we engage subjects for research study."

He swallowed hard, knowing that the discussion was finally steering toward him.

"Private, your immediate response, yesterday, saved the lives of most of your unit. You should consider yourself a hero; the ability you've feared all of your life has proven its potential for greatness. You should be very proud of that fact and of yourself. Now, I am pleased to tell you that your enlistment has been modified."

Feelings of both joy and guilt filled his heart, soul, and mind. He would be going home because of his ability, but that didn't relieve the countless number of his peers.

"Oh, but you won't be going home, at least not yet anyway."

Foster had read his mind. He did say he was telepathic...didn't he? Prior feelings turned to both angst and curiosity.

"I have been appointed to take you back to Washington with me, where you will become a subject of our remote hearing study in exchange for your draft time here. It really isn't such a bad deal, Private. You won't have to serve in this war, worrying about your life every day and night, seeing your fellow soldiers being blown to bits and pieces, imagining yourself going home one day. With our offer, you *will* be going home one day."

He would recall the look of certainty and truth on Foster's face for years to come. The guilt inside him stirred, but the thought of being studied, being able to understand at last, and then being able to go home, back to her, was greater.

He gave a silent affirmation with a nod of his head.

"Then it's settled. We leave here, immediately."

That decision had sealed his fate forever.

* * * *

The plane ride was a long one, and now from the back window of an unmarked black sedan, the nation's capital sprawled out before him in its official splendor. Historical monuments stood proudly, cherry blossoms lined the famous avenues, and protesters marched upon the capital with signs that read *Make Love Not War*, as well as the popular plea calling for *Cease Fire*.

The official seat of the United States was a great relief and a predictable culture shock from the flat terrain of the land and the overflowing foliage of the South Vietnamese jungles. This new scenario loomed large before him, ushering him to the forefront of a pending and undeclared history.

The shouts of the protesters reverberated through the glass, representing a movement of which he would not directly be involved. The sedan rolled through the boulevards, oblivious to the blooming chaos of its surroundings. Suddenly, the car made a sharp right-turn into a tunnel, and overhead, darkness fell upon the discreet vehicle, interrupted only by the fluorescent tubes strung along the tunnel's upper walls that shone a sleeker black on the sedan as it entered.

Then the car stopped abruptly.

A few seconds had passed before one of the agents in front opened the passenger door for him; the other agent stood behind, near the wheel of the passenger's side.

"Right this way." The agent who had opened the door instructed him, and he followed, flanked on both sides by the escorting emissaries. They walked to what looked like a security elevator within the tunnel, and the first agent keyed a lock with a clockwise motion, and then pressed a button on the wall panel. A *whooshing* sound from underground shot upward to his ears.

It was déjà vu as the elevator doors opened wide for him like giant, metal jaws. The three of them stepped inside, and the deep, downward drop of the small entrapment caused the familiar clogging of his ears. The agents had stayed silent and so had he. He had learned not to ask them questions. They wouldn't answer, even if they knew.

The doors opened, revealing another underground facility, only this one was cleaner, brighter, constructed more like a high-tech, communications center, and by appearance, that's exactly what it was.

Computer systems he had never seen before were set up like small work stations, equipped with radar and visual screens, audio and recording apparatus, and a network of blinking red, blue, and green lights that beamed through the dimness like Christmas displays. The machines had voices of their own, bleeping, blurting noises beckoning brightly for attention, somehow alive, yet the stations stood unmanned.

The purpose and the extent of this vast array of technology would remain a mystery to him for now because here in this clandestine underground, the translation of top-secret meant unmentioned and unheard.

His escorts eased away as Agent Foster and two others approached.

"Welcome, Private. Our journey was a long one, but I see you've had the chance to unwind and refresh a bit."

Foster's voice echoed softly through the underground. He was accompanied by a bald and muscle-bound brute whose unnatural biceps bulged in steroidal bliss; his crystal blue eyes seemed to pierce the young Private where he stood. The other was a woman of about fifty, her face a stony attractiveness, and gray streaked through her once dark hair that was pulled backward in a bun.

"Allow me to introduce you," Foster said, his hand motioning backward. "This is Caleb; he is our most renowned remote-viewer. His performance has been most exemplary, seeing things remotely all over the world with amazing accuracy, including, Private, the far-away war which you have just left behind."

The muscled giant nodded his head in introduction; the look on his face was softer, but still seemingly intent, watchful with a fire that burned behind blue eyes. With the same hand, Foster motioned again, this time to the woman, stone-faced with the slightest hint of a smile, her black turtleneck wrapped tightly to her torso like a uniform.

"And this is Myra," he said, as the staunch woman nodded. "She is a clairaudient listener, much like you. She is also a telepath with the keenest ability to gain insight into the minds of others, so watch your thoughts."

Foster laughed at this with a joking gesture meant to ease the young Private; his cohorts mimicked his hospitality.

"You will be able to learn from the both of them, as they will you. They will be your mentors. I am convinced that once you have the chance to study and to test your ability to the fullest capacity, you will come to understand and even appreciate it. Relax, Private, here you will be safe from the rigors of war."

He slipped into relief, but still something sinister stirred inside of him. He wished he'd known back then what he knew today.

* * * *

As the vibe of suspicion failed to dwindle, he began asking questions about home before the testing ever began: did his family know he was here? How often could he call home? Did *she* know he was here? Abrupt and slightly manufactured answers had greeted him.

"No, Private, as we told you, this operation is top-secret, classified. Your family, as well as your young lady, thinks you are still fighting in the jungles. You will be allowed to write them, as you usually do, but you will be instructed on how to maintain your cover to them, as though you are still halfway around the world. The postmarks will confirm that. Obviously, phone calls are not an option."

The expected twinge of disappointment disappeared as he began to understand. Besides, he didn't want his family knowing that he was indulging the same ability they had so deeply shunned in his life. He agreed, and the testing began.

The sessions were always behind closed, soundproof doors of small rooms, where he would be made to either stretch out on the couch like a Psych patient, or sit upright facing away from the door, listening for sounds from elsewhere's unknown.

At first, they had taped wires and pulse pad electrodes to his temples, reading brain waves, and testing his normal senses to gain a clearer picture of his brain function. Once that had been concluded, he began testing with Myra. He'd sat with her for hours, trying to pick the magic word she was thinking from her closed mind; five times out of ten, he had done so. Then, she would leave the room, walk a lengthy distance away to the opposite end of the vast underground, and read aloud an Almanac listing for a famous date in history.

When she returned, she had expected his answer to her question: to what date had she referred? He watched her slight smile widen with pride when he answered her correctly.

"April 15, 1865."

How ironically thrilled she'd been to hear of the Lincoln assassination.

More and more he felt like a Guinea pig, but the need to understand, and the hope of going home urged him onward. Going home, that was what drove him. He did exactly as they wanted, whenever they wanted.

He worked faster with the testing as the incentives danced in his anxious heart, and the images invaded his mind. He kept picturing her beautiful face and long blond hair, hearing her laugh, and remembering how she had grabbed on to him when his number was called out.

He envisioned a new life with her and all of this behind him.

But he would immediately snap out of those thoughts to focus on the tasks at hand. The sooner he finished, the sooner he would be on his way home—or so he thought.

He'd spent most of his days and nights in the underground compound, and when his work was over, guards would return him to an above ground barracks where he was housed. He was not permitted to leave the barracks for any means as he'd been stressed upon how important it was in maintaining his cover. So young and naively he'd believed, dreaming and reading within his small encampment when the long day's tasks had been completed.

The changes he'd witnessed outside of his one lonely window were the only indicators of how the months had turned to seasons. The leaves had changed to brilliant red, yellow, and orange hues, swaying and falling to the strong autumn breeze, and night fell early now, as the last few hours of daylight were gone by the time he was escorted back to his barracks from the underground.

He was now encouraged to utilize his listening ability at his own will. He was taught how to relax, search his mind, focus, and then reach out. They'd given him certain locations and he would focus, honing in on some word that was given him, reaching out for the slightest word, sentence, or audible voice that he could retrieve.

Apparently, he didn't disappoint, though repeating what he'd picked up like radar still did not enable him to understand what he was hearing or "listening" to. He retrieved phrases like "power supply," "special aircraft," "inside investigation," then became more specific, naming planned dates and times snatched unseen from secret conversations. None of this held any interest for him. He thought of only her, his family, and his friends left behind in a bloody war he'd escaped.

Agent Foster and Myra often glanced at each other in what seemed like instant recognition when he would recite all that he'd heard, but there was something else he'd noticed, something peculiar. They would stare at each other for several moments, as though some secretive form of communication co-existed between them. It was not long before he realized that they were speaking telepathically, avoiding the possibility that he might overhear them with either his true ear, or his ability that they had so adamantly enabled.

What were they hiding? The thought crept into his mind with a growing frequency, and he remembered what Foster had said about his cloaking his mind. The more he thought about it, the more he realized that he was also able to perform this task; after all, wasn't his ability the reason why he was here?

He taught himself a few tricks, allowing his mind to go blank, focusing his attention on some object: a light switch, the elevator, the machines, or the large, square screen that had remained black, inactive, since the day he entered this concealed facility. He erected a defensive guard around him, cloaking his thoughts as they had cloaked theirs.

If they could hide, he could hide also.

Something was changing; something was going down. He refused to be a Guinea pig any longer. It was the next day when he sat in a one-on-one meeting with Myra. As she looked at him, that hidden smile of hers became more and more apparent, displaying a certain pride for an emerging prized pupil.

"Private, you have done extremely well with your testing here. We have been able to fully document the extent of your ability, as well as the progress you have made in strengthening it. I trust that you are going to become a much needed factor in the course of our objectives, congratulations." Her smile seemed awkward.

A much needed factor? Slight anxiety tweaked inside him, causing an inner rush of urgency. What did she mean? When would he be leaving? Quickly he quashed these emotions and thoughts, fighting hard and as he did so, letting his mind go blank, focusing on her smile, even mimicking the suspicious grin. She continued her praise of him, unaware.

This time, no deafness came upon him before he'd heard. Her inner thoughts became unwilling insertions into his mind...

Now, how do we stray his thoughts from returning home? He can't find out...

The unexpected interruption sent a jolt through him, but she failed to notice his fast-frightened movement that nearly bolted him from the chair. He stopped and remained calm. He stared back at her, wondering if she knew that he'd read her mind.

"So, Agent Foster and I will be holding a conference pertaining to your work with us. I have been asked to give a progress report on my testing with you. I am sure everyone will be as pleased as I am with the results."

She rose from the chair, concluding the meeting. His lips parted to speak, but *now* the deafness overcame him. Her back had been turned when the voice of a posthumous, higher-ranking officer stole his ear...

"Remain silent, Private! Don't ask about home!"

The deafness left him quickly, and his broken heart beat loudly. Myra left the room, oblivious to her error.

* * * *

It was in this room that he'd remained silent as ordered by his ghostly superior, though the inner inkling to flee had intensified with a final certainty. That familiar, automatic knowledge instructed him to sit and await his next move, while the surety of danger now manifested in a sweat that washed over his face and body, and the feeling of time ticking away had caused a readied mental watch for an unknown, crucial moment.

The door of this room, like most, contained a rectangular window, and through it, he shifted his eyes as far left as possible. It was from that direction that he caught a limited view of Foster, Caleb, and Myra marching up the hallway and turning into the room just before this one. They're in the room next door, he thought, realizing with that recurring sense of urgency that the meeting was about him.

The walls and doors were soundproof in this place, yet it wouldn't matter to a clairaudient whose ability had now been perfected. He knew they were aware of this; after all, his flourishing ability was the subject of the meeting. He felt certain that they would be speaking telepathically, a meeting of the minds, mind to mind, so to speak. But Myra had missed the fact that his own telepathy had forced its way to the forefront, a crucial factor that Foster would not have overlooked.

Instinctively, he drew back from the window. Quick shadows interrupting the light against the opposite wall told him that the door to the next room had been opened then closed. He gasped hard and sat back down, bringing the chair toward the wall. He closed his eyes hard and honed his mental ear, knowing what he had to do.

His instinct had been right. As the deafness numbed his ears, no voices could be heard from inside the small room next door. They had been communicating telepathically, insuring that he would not overhear. Caleb was also in that room—why? He was a remote viewer. Was he watching him?

He threw his head back and exhaled, opened his eyes, and stared at the ceiling. Then with his mind, he refocused as the deafness died away. He allowed a natural calm to wash over him, and concentrated on the wall that separated them. Voices broke through, exposing random thoughts like camouflaged enemies.

"Is he telepathic?"

It was Foster. His words were thick in a soft, surrounding silence, but unmistakably, he'd asked the question about him. A lengthy pause had followed before the next voice invaded his mind.

"Very little...has an undeveloped talent for telepathy."

The words were fast, fleeting, fading, but it was the voice of Myra explaining that he, the subject, was not a developed enough telepath for the goals at hand...

She'd made a serious and fatal blunder.

His crafty deception of her had been successful; he'd figured it out through Foster's mistake of mentioning thought cloaking. He had managed to avoid her more experienced telepathic mind as it searched for signs that could ultimately threaten their plans. Her voice was heard again, referring to the testing in which he'd pulled words from her mind.

"Only scored five of ten...capable...not strong enough. Powerful listener, though. He's clairaudient...highest capacity."

He listened as Foster's response confirmed his suspicions.

"Cannot leave here...he's needed for our efforts...next part of the plan..."

"What if he resists?" Myra's tone was skeptical.

"There are ways..."

Foster's scattered words continued, and the words that came next, though broken, triggered his alarm like the day at the bridge.

"We are not the FBI...have to move fast...before...find us...rogues...treason."

Shock struck him, terror gripped him, and disbelief had stumped him. This unexpected revelation incited everything he'd felt on the battlefield, all over again, and the slightest strain of rage caused his mind to dance along the edge of insanity. His blood stirred and boiled, while raw, ripened nerves caused his body tremors. They were not the FBI;

they were a highly sophisticated, psychically intelligent rogue group, and they had kidnapped him.

Kidnappers...and they had plucked him away from his enlistment right under the government's eye...but how? At first, Foster spoke of the government's psychic studies of remote vision and hearing, and how they would be used towards issues of national defense, but then...

The powers that be, however, are beginning to shun the results of our efforts...

Both Foster and his team were either rejects dismissed from the government's studies, or else the whole project had been shut down. The elder agent had struck him as an outsider from the very beginning. Why hadn't he trusted his instincts?

Now they were planning on stealing him away from his home, his family, and the love of his life, capitalizing on his abilities, utilizing him as a psychic Guinea pig, an unwitting slave to their secretive game of paranormal espionage.

He closed his eyes in helplessness; then he suddenly jolted as a pair of crystal blue eyes peered back at him through that momentary darkness.

Caleb *was* watching him from the other room!

He closed his eyes again, and still, the perfect crystalline orbs of brilliant blue gazed back. He could even make out the sinister, pointed arch of the shapely, blond eyebrows. Quickly, he abandoned the feelings of fear and helplessness in favor of a newfound sense of empowerment that had overtaken him. Now he not only gazed back at those eyes, but through them.

And so easily, he slipped inside Caleb's mind.

A quick picture of Caleb's brain flashed before him, and then the eyes appeared again, only somehow strained. His new telepathic talent had turned into a toy, and with it, he playfully reached further into the recesses of Caleb's mind.

"Something's wrong!" He heard the bulging hulk give a weakened gasp and speak with a slight tremor in his voice.

His mind like a battering ram, he gave one final push into Caleb's mental barricade. He saw a vision of himself, as though he were staring in the mirror.

The eyes returned, peering upward in a heightened state of fear. He watched as blood vessels climbed like ivies across the whites of the eyes and burst behind the blue orbs. A slight phantom pain mimicked in his own eyes.

"AAAHHH!"

The scream had come from Caleb. This time he'd heard it with his naked ear through the so-called, soundproof wall. Slowly, he backed with baby steps away from the wall, uncertain of what had occurred beyond it. If something happened to Caleb while he remotely watched him, then they must be on to him or at least close.

There was only one exit from this room, yet his head turned in multiple directions, scanning and searching for a way out. Safety and security had now slipped away unexpectedly. He had to make a break from this place even if they killed him; they were going to take his life one way or the other.

He ran to the door, the nervous sweat drenching his face, and his heart pounding a hard and rapid percussion. The door had been locked as expected; it was his only shot, but the steel knob failed to twist in either direction. Even if it would've opened, where would he run? They'd blindfolded him before they brought him here, but he was a soldier now; he would die finding his way out if he had to.

Rising voices could be heard. He strained his eyes to see through the small window in the door, detecting only moving shadows that danced down the corridor. Approaching sounds came closer to the room, and the dancing shadows interrupted the light outside once again.

Abruptly the deafness came, and the voice of the fallen superior shouted this time, instructing him as before.

"Private, step away from the door! Be prepared!"

No other words were spoken. His hearing returned, somehow sharper. The sounds were coming for him, and he was told to be prepared.

A face appeared in the rectangular window of the door, displaying a stunned yet determined expression; it was Foster's. Was Foster whom he was to be prepared for? What was he going to do? What had happened? He couldn't know, but he knew one thing as the conversation he'd overheard continued to replay in his mind; he would have to kill Foster to leave here, and as the fury spread inside him, he now felt prepared.

* * * *

Foster pushed the door open and let it fly back, then steadily strode into the room, his intent gaze staring straight into his eyes.

"Well, it looks like you've accomplished much more in your time here than we'd originally anticipated. Your talent for telepathy seems to have evaded Myra, but not Caleb, but I must admit, you managed to slip past even me."

Foster ogled him for a silent moment, searching his mind and sporting a maddening grin that spread across his face. In the intensity of the previous moments, he'd forgotten to shut down his thoughts.

"Yes, my little slip of the tongue about thought cloaking—how stupid of me. That is, of course, how you fooled Myra. What we weren't aware of is your heightened state of telepathy; nor did we envision your rare capability of entering and invading the mind of another. Those with such a unique ability have been known to cause severe damage and destruction, which you have just unwittingly demonstrated. You see, Private, you have an extremely powerful psychic instrument. One which, unfortunately, we cannot afford."

His eyes widened as Foster pulled a revolver from his inner jacket pocket and pointed it straight at him. But he remained alert, treating the agent like a preying tiger, though Foster stood still, making no sudden moves. Without actually forming the words in his mind, he had the notion of talking to Foster, stalling him, hopefully distracting him.

"What do you mean destruction? What happened to Caleb?"

"Caleb is dead, my friend, no thanks to you."

The automatic recognition surged inside of him; he'd gone too far.

"Those who are unable to understand or control that little unspeakable capability can cause great damage, as I said. As was explained to you before, clairaudience is a form of telepathy, though not all listeners are capable of telepathy. In some, it remains hidden for years, dormant for decades, possibly even the rest of their lives. But, you, Private, developed your telepathic sense to its fullest, just by our provoking it. And with it, came that ability so rarely accomplishable in others. This, we had not expected.

"You entered Caleb's mind as he was remotely viewing you. You already know this, of course. He fell to the floor, blinded and bleeding by your intrusive handiwork. From what we have been able to ascertain, he suffered a massive hemorrhaging to the brain, dying instantly."

Deep inside of him, he knew that this was not his intention. He wasn't trying to kill Caleb, only to reach out to discover what was going on.

"We are well aware that it was unintentional"

He shut down his thoughts and let Foster's voice echo through his ears.

"But you must understand, you are now a liability to us. You are a danger not only to us, but to yourself. If the powers that be discover your newfound ability, how long do you think they will let you live? I am actually doing you a favor, Private."

"You had no intention of allowing me to leave here!"

"Well, that may be true. I am sure you overheard everything. That is the reason why you are no longer of use to us. The tables have turned on us; you are a more powerful psychic being than we had assumed. We cannot work with a subject who will purposefully thwart our efforts. Our cover has been blown, as they say, with you."

"There's only one thing I don't understand," he said, keeping his eyes closely on Foster's hand and slowly sidestepping his position away from it. The two men began to move in circles around each other. "You claimed to be the FBI, but now I know you're not. So, who the hell are you?"

"We once belonged to the FBI and their remote psychic study project. One might say I'm a 'former' agent. Those whom I refer to as 'the powers that be' became disinterested with our methods of study. They wanted to take the project to a lesser level than what we were undertaking, baby steps, so to speak. Our studies had thrived too much to be extinguished; that is why we have broken away from the government and its projects to advance our own."

"But the Bureau will be on to you." He began filling in the missing pieces that Foster failed to provide. "Your failure with me is bound to lead them to you, eventually."

"Your hidden telepathy is evenly matched against your clairaudience, Private. It is a shame that you don't find yourself on the same side with us, that you remain attached to familial ties. You could have been a powerful asset. I see no need, Private, to waste any more of our time together."

Foster stepped closer to him, while he continued his steady sidestepping footwork, a slowly moving target distracting his would-be shooter. He could almost feel steam seeping from his body, a result of his boiling blood. The notion that Foster was going to kill him erected with hardened, concrete certainty. He was going to have to move fast because either he, or Foster, was going to die today.

The voice of the fellow superior officer spoke again...

"Be ready, Private."

Foster tightened his grip on the revolver, his finger forming a squeeze around the trigger. He saw a slight expression of regret form on Foster's face, seemingly aware of the ghostly guide that spoke—but not to him. And then in his mind, the soldier heard the words that had unleashed Hell on the other side of the world...

"Tan cong!"

Something snapped inside him. The fear from the far away jungle had returned with a newfound rage recently accumulated and never released—until now. He bellowed in a wild, untamed caterwaul as he rushed Foster full-force with his body. He managed to catch the right hand, which held the revolver, pinning Foster's thumb down into the wrist muscle. Then with his right shoulder, he rammed the older man against the wall with a heavy thud.

Foster gasped from the impact, so he squeezed the hand holding the revolver even harder. Still clenching the subdued hand, he rocked him backward then forward against the wall, harder, slamming him over and over as he was, in many ways, the unseen enemy. He heard a solid knock as Foster hit his head upon the wall, and his deadly grip on the gun loosened.

He wriggled his fingers against the cold steel until he disentangled the frantic, fidgeting fingers that gripped it. Now the cold steel quenched the grimy sweat of his palm as he'd strategically stolen the weapon away. He stopped for only a second as Foster breathed in heavy gasps.

He was in control now, but Foster made the mistake of rushing back at him.

No further thought was needed when he pulled the trigger, and the small explosion magnified throughout the small room. It was all so fast.

He wasn't even sure he'd hit the elder agent until he saw the gaping, fifty-cent piece sized hole that formed a canal in his chest. The blood was reddening his white shirt beneath the jacket as he stumbled backward a few steps. A mask of disbelief hardened on Foster's face as he fell to the floor; the final table had been turned on him. His blood flowed fast, soaking his clothes. Then there was a gasp, a gurgle, then silence.

He searched to find a sense of relief in this final moment and failed.

Newly infused fear and paranoia from entrapment and confinement surged within him, turning him wild. He hadn't wanted this, but it was either him or Foster, and he was intent on surviving.

His breathing was heavy as he ran to the door. Foster had closed it again, and again, it remained locked. He pointed the revolver at the stubborn steel knob and blasted it into oblivion, replacing it with a black gaping hole that blew the door backwards.

He stepped out into the underground corridor that seemed deserted, silenced of the few random voices that had filled it. He could still hear the bleeps and blurbs of the machines. The doorway to the room where they'd held the meeting stood open, and he stared inside. A fresh puddle of blood soaked the floor, and the acrid, sticky smell of it wafted to his nostrils.

It was Caleb's blood. He wondered what he had done to him. Would he ever know? What about Myra? Where was she?

He had no sooner thought about her when he'd heard a weak *kiai* of attack behind him and felt a hard, yet insignificant, thud against the back of his head and shoulders. He'd turned to find her rabid fear confronting him, her face wild, her eyes wide and her intent vengeful.

It was impulse that caused him to pull the trigger this time. The blast did not take her by surprise as it had Foster. She wilted like a broken willow against the floor, her hand covering the hole in her abdomen. He watched as she died, and the feeling of being alone in this abandoned underground allowed him to think, if only for minutes.

Where were the guards? He remained alert, ready to fire again. He reached out, honing his mental ear...no sounds approached.

He walked through the cool underground, facing the machines with their bright, blinking splendor, as they were the only sounds to be heard. Then a fast, whirring sound turned him around to face the square screen that had remained blank and devoid of life or images the entire time he'd been there.

Tiny gray specks of static danced and developed into a forming image on what now loomed like a rare, enlarged, television screen. The image showed an elderly man with a storm of white hair, watching him where he stood. He had never seen him before, but the man stared back at him with what appeared to be not only recognition, but lack of surprise, and almost contentment.

The man spoke while looking directly down at him, examining his every move, as though he were a bug.

"Congratulations, Private! You have done amazingly well. You have completed your course of studies far better than our expectations!"

"Who are you?" he asked.

"Who I am is not important. It is who *you* are going to be that is our greatest accomplishment. Please, do come closer. I cannot bite, as you can see." A wry, congested laugh escaped the old man.

He moved even closer to the screen.

"As I have said, well done, Private."

"How? What do you mean?"

"I have been watching you for quite some time, knowing all along that you would make a far more effective psychic research tool than either Foster or Myra."

Instantly, he thought back to the glass wall in the underground room he was taken to before being brought here, that ominous feeling of someone watching from behind it.

"You're right, Private. Your talents serve you well."

"So, you're the brains behind this rogue group, not Foster?"

"That's correct. Everyone answers to a superior don't they? Foster, Myra, Caleb, all workers remitting to a higher establishment. I am the leader and overseer of this clandestine project, one that has mutinied with our government in effort to achieve success of the highest order. We have found the possibility of that success in you, young man."

He felt the need to run, but to where? He looked around once again for the guards.

"The guards have been directed not to apprehend you, Private, that is, unless you intend on leaving here so soon...relax." Something about the elder man's tone grew darker. So, he was another telepath. How many were there within this cryptic and illicit organization?

"Of all of our many varied and covert associates, young man, you have proven yourself to be by far, the strongest, the most receptive, and the most effective. And yes, I am also a telepathic clairaudient, not quite as strong as you in my day, but of the highest form. Needless to say, most of my abilities have dwindled with age. The demonstration of *your* abilities upon poor Caleb was quite impressive."

"I never meant to—"

"Good riddance, Private...irrelevant."

So someone else's life was irrelevant waged next to their goals.

"What do you want with me?" He spoke as his head was directed up at the screen, asking the question in vain, already knowing the answer.

"You are going to take over for me, Private, when the time comes." He closed his eyes softly at the further mention of his advancing age. "With you, we can achieve so much more with one mind than our efforts of so many combined. The FBI had abandoned this operation to further their more mundane approaches. We will soon establish our efforts as superior with you at the helm of this operation."

The old man on the screen read his thoughts before he had time to form them.

"Our motives? Our motives are simple: a highly effective state of world security. Imagine a world where wars have been eliminated because we have read our enemies' minds beforehand, overheard their strategic plotting down to the minutest detail, or seen their actions remotely from a great distance. Such great achievements of our national defense would become outstanding accomplishments on the part of highly enabled psychic paragons such as you."

Even then, he felt there was more, but this time he buried his thoughts carefully.

"And if I refuse?"

The man looked in closer from beyond the screen.

"You cannot refuse us, Private. After all, you are a murderer now, aren't you?"

"Foster was—"

"Yes, Foster was trying to kill you, Private. But can you prove that? Then there is the issue of Myra. She was an unarmed woman who may have been defending herself, that is, until you shot her. You see, Private, we can expose each other. You were a young soldier taken straight from this hideous war by your own consent, and then you went haywire during our illegal research. You lost your mind, Private. You killed people.

"So, you see, it is either their prison, or ours. Besides, we know where your family is, and yes, we know about *her*. Distractions can be dealt with quite effectively."

He felt both his heart and his soul sink somewhere into oblivion. Then there was the issue of what had occurred in Nam, overhearing the plans for sneak attack. He would have to explain, but would anyone believe him? What if they tried to implicate him in some way? What if they tried to paint him as a lunatic even though he could prove his abilities?

"That's just it," the man continued. "Do you really want to expose your family, and her, to this alarming ability that has now come to the forefront of your life? Do you think they could tolerate it? What about her...what would your ability mean to her life? I'm sure you're aware that psychic abilities of this nature are often heredity. Was having children part of your plans, Private? Would they end up forgiving such an inheritance?"

"Shut up!" In the flush of anger he felt rushed, confused. He had no doubt that they would harm his family, all of them, including her. Dangerous minds were at work, and if he didn't comply, they might kill him, *and* them. He had no choice; he would have to play their game at least for a while. There would have to be a way out, somehow, sometime, but right now, there was no escaping this psychic band of terrorists.

"That may someday be possible, but within moments, your family will receive word that you have been reported MIA. After all, your superiors were unaware of what happened to you the night you were brought here."

All of it had been an elaborate abduction.

"You will be given a whole new identity, and of course, you will be awarded a life of considerable financial compensation for your allegiance. You're about to become a very rich man, never wanting for anything."

...Except for her, his family, and his friends.

Fear had frozen him solid. He would have given anything to be back on that bridge right now or back in the jungles fighting fiercely for his country, anywhere but this nightmare that began to settle in like an unforeseen storm. He couldn't let them harm his family or her; he wouldn't let that happen.

He looked up into the dark, aged eyes on the screen and then lowered his own eyes and head in defeated consent. Satisfaction bellowed from the old man's elated voice.

"Excellent choice, Private, and I assure you, you won't regret it."

He sank to the floor and felt part of his soul slip away...forever.

* * * *

The screen had faded back to black, and he'd sat alone for hours, listening to nothing but the sounds of the machines. He'd slumped, immovable, into a random chair within a small cubicle, the aches from his exhausted body kicking in the lull of endorphins. His mind was clouded, cluttered, confused; he could hear nothing if he tried, only the machines. Today, lives were lost, threatened, and altered forever, the chaotic turmoil of which, left him spent and speechless.

He was roused from the drifting reverie by the sound of the elevator doors as they opened. The two familiar guards neared him, only this time with expressions of almost friendliness, hospitality.

"Right this way, Sir."

Sir, why had they called him "Sir?"

So suddenly, everything had changed, as though he'd killed the witch with a bucket of cold water. They escorted him out of the underground and into an awaiting limo, and the door was slammed shut by the chauffeuring guard. He sat back and let his mind go blank, a technique he would soon need to master.

The drive took thirty minutes, after which, the guards led him up to a plush, private penthouse. The spacious accommodation had new, light-blue, shag carpeting with stylish, modern furniture in the living room, as well as a kitchen, an office, a large master bedroom, two bathrooms, and a balcony displaying a magnificent oceanfront view.

"Who am I waiting for, him?" He asked the guards in a more poignant tone.

"No, this is your home now, Sir. You will find everything you need in your office."

So, this was one of his compensations? After everything they'd done to him, he still found it hard to hate the immediate surroundings as he looked around the spacious suite. He turned and saw the guards leaving.

"Wait, what am I supposed to do?"

"As we said, Sir, you will find everything you need inside the office. This is your penthouse; everything in here belongs to you." As the guards descended in the suite's elevator, the silence of a new life greeted him expectantly. He found the office down the hall, first door on the left-hand side.

Against the wall was another screen like the other, though black for now. A large desk sat opposite the screen, and oak bookshelves lined the walls. He sat down at the desk and slowly, cautiously, opened the drawer.

Inside he found a passport, a forged birth certificate, and a driver's license. He placed the contents upon the desk and examined them. The pictures on the corresponding ID's were of him, only the name didn't match, and now for the first time, he was introduced to his new identity. He looked down at his new name underneath headshots they had taken of him in the beginning.

Roman Paul Hadley; Annapolis, Maryland.

So that was his new name: Roman Hadley. What if someone, somewhere, sometime, recognized him? Did they consider that?

Just as he sat contemplating, the black screen turned on, and an image of the old man appeared, uninvited.

"Congratulations, Roman. You're a new man now. As I'm sure you've gladly gathered I will no longer be calling you Private. I trust you've found your surroundings most comfortable?"

He stared at the screen with contempt.

"That's okay, we will become fast friends; I assure you. If you look in the drawer to your right, you will find all that you need, and more will be supplied to you."

He opened the drawer, and the greenish-gray splendor greeted him seductively. He pulled the wads out of hiding and placed them in front of him.

"You may count it if you like. It's all yours."

The wadded piles of hundreds, fifties, and twenties packed the drawer full, and as he touched it, the smell of freshly minted cash assailed his nostrils.

"There is two-hundred and fifty-thousand dollars. You will receive another payment in three months. You have no bills, my friend; your accommodations are seen to. You may live in comfort as you see fit."

He looked at another ID card he'd failed to recognize at first. It was a Federal Bureau of Investigation badge, and he, Roman Hadley, was listed as a special agent.

"So, wait, I work for the FBI?" He was confused even more.

"You work for us, Mr. Hadley. Your identification as a special agent is your cover, a very convenient cover."

"But how can you continue to masquerade as the Bureau when—"

"Right under their noses, Mr. Hadley, we have been doing so for quite some time. You will exist as Roman Hadley, and we will handle the rest."

And so he passed the years as Roman Hadley, the wealthy and

reclusive Roman Hadley. In the first of those few years, he utilized his ability in countless covert projects, listening remotely to distant hijacking plots, assassination plans, corrupt politicians, even a scandal that had enveloped the White House. Later, the focus had geared toward issues of security, listening to plans and directives, new ideas and advancements, and reporting all that he'd secretly overheard back to the group.

These various pieces of information were compiled and fed into the database of the machines he'd seen in the underground, which were then stored, reproduced, and then examined to search for sensible patterns that could make logical predictions. It was around that time in 1974 when the man behind the screen was no more, and his assignment to succeed had begun.

He had never known the man's name...

"It is better that you remain unaware; you will refer to me as 'Z,'" the old man had replied, when he boldly asked. It was of no consequence now; the man was dead and now he was in charge. He would stifle his thoughts into silence toward the group's remaining underling telepaths and work fast to find an escape plan.

But that was not to be had.

All documents and information regarding the rogue group and its illegal operations named Roman Hadley as the chief investigator, the leading investigative power behind the project. He'd been the fall guy in an elaborate strategy. The old man had framed him even before he died, associating the entire operation to the fictitious identity forcefully bestowed upon him, and then conveniently leaving him in charge of the unwanted legacy. If discovered, he faced any number of federal charges including criminal conspiracy, treason, espionage, even murder.

In 1976, the rogue group received news that the FBI had disbanded their remote psychic research projects. This had caused a stir among the group because the cover that served as a mirror operation was now blown and non-existent, yet he was not hopeful for a way out; all indicators pointed to him, and even though he served at the helm, the threat toward his loved ones still remained in effect.

Some hidden source of authority had anonymously threatened him. Z had obviously not worked alone; he was only one of many players in this dangerous game. He had known this much, for this unknown source had continued his compensation. Accepting it all of these years had made him feel even guiltier.

He continued the group's research projects as a low-key, psychic investigative group. No mention of the FBI would ever be made again. Silently, he went on searching and plotting in his mind any possible exit strategies, but years had turned to decades, and hope finally led to acceptance.

The remote viewers would find him soon enough if he disappeared. There was one absolute way out, but every time he looked at the revolver he kept in his desk drawer, he thought of her and the hope that he might see her again one day. There was also the fear of surviving the bullet to the brain and trading one Hell for another, or thinking on it so much that one of the many telepaths in this operation would expose him.

One of the group's many functions was discovering telepaths around the country and tracking them telepathically through channeling. That's what the blinking lights on the map in the underground had been: tracking indicators used by remote viewers and listeners, representing the physical presences of those for whom they watched and listened.

He had learned of Sidney Pratt when the young man was only a boy, a very highly effective listener who could hear the dead with an ability that was biblically resonant. Then unexpectedly, the young boy had led him to *her*. It was a sign. He'd entered young Sidney's mind several times but then desisted, remembering what had happened to Caleb.

He bided more years until Sidney Pratt became a member of the elite and nationally recognized Paranormal Research and Investigative society at his university. Roman Hadley quickly found himself a seat on the board of directors. But the young group would never meet him in person; he kept tabs on them telepathically, especially Sidney, but he would remain unseen. They were also unaware of his location whether it be in Pittsburgh, Chicago, New York, London, or any of the various places he easily frequented around the world.

Then through a strange and tragic coincidence, the connection Sidney had to *her* had suddenly been re-established. His sign had returned. What if Sidney Pratt was a powerful enough clairaudient to take over where Roman Hadley had once been?

But as Hadley gently entered Sidney's mind, he realized that the young man's telepathic ability was miniscule; he was capable of hearing the dead, not the living. But Sidney had led him to another option, one more powerful than he had ever known, even himself—Ryan Quinn.

The young boy was powerful enough to channel Sidney's dormant telepathy and be heard. He suspected that Ryan Quinn could even possess the same rare ability that he himself possessed, entering the minds of others. He'd waited years for such a find.

But now his entire past was returning to haunt him as life's events assembled together on an unstable fault line, quaking before a climactic eruption. As he continued to gaze out the window reliving the past, words from the present formed in his telepathic mind. He redialed the number on his private cell and spoke again.

"He's on his way to the hospital. Find him!"

Again, he didn't wait for an answer as he slammed the cell shut. His heart began to drum an incessant pounding as a slight anxiety crept slowly through his veins. Everything was now coming to the forefront after all of these years. Like the first strategic move on an elaborate chessboard, his plan of escaping this nightmare had been placed in motion.

He had just given the order to kidnap Ryan Quinn, and this bold, instinctive move would determine both of their fates...forever.

Chapter Five

The steady rhythm of the car soothed her anger down to disappointment as she drove to the hospital, diverting her eyes to the street sides in search of her son. She realized why he'd taken off like that: because he knew she wouldn't drive him. She had wanted him to stay away from those investigators, and none of them understood why.

What was so important that he had to tell Sidney Pratt? Did it concern his father, and if so, why wouldn't he come to her? But, she knew the obvious answers to these questions. She had discouraged this ability from the onset, even making a deal with him that she feared he couldn't possibly keep.

The guilt she sometimes felt was an unwelcome and recurring visitor whose face she'd slammed the door on many times. Now, that decision began to haunt her, and she found herself being forced from the denial she'd become so comfortable in. The secret of Ryan's father stirred inside of her, and silently she knew she couldn't keep it hidden much longer; Ryan's ability was becoming stronger.

She had lied to the investigators when she claimed not to know where his ability came from. Well, she spoke a half-truth; it *didn't* come from her. Ian, Ryan's father, was a different story...

Those sage-green eyes had attracted her long before she knew the truth about what kind of person lived behind them. In their younger days, he seemed like such an easy-going guy, a hard worker, and honest. He was a strong, strapping, Irish-American lad with reddish brown hair and enigmatic eyes she couldn't ignore, and as they became closer, she felt like she could follow him anywhere.

They shacked up, as her mother called it, but those seemed like the good times. Then she got pregnant, and things slowly changed. She knew that Ian felt cornered, as Ryan was unexpected, but he loved him to death...literally. Under the mounting pressure of the enormous life change, not to mention the rising finances, Ian began drinking heavily.

He'd always drunk socially, but it became ongoing, bringing with it a domineering and possessive personality that overtook him. He was not the same man that once caused her heart to skip. He began coming home later, drunker, and meaner. Soon, it was he who threw the first punch when one night, well past midnight, a backhand struck the side of her face, stunning her into silent shock.

He'd flung a little-too-late dinner plate into the air, sending bites of beef, rice, and potatoes flying across the room to cling to the curtains, windows, and walls.

"How am I supposed to eat this? It's cold!" His voice was a drunken roar she'd prayed her son wouldn't hear. His temper had been building, but she had never seen him like this, his face turning the same shade as his bloodshot eyes. She eased the sharp sting of the right side of her face with the cold palm of her hand, and then in her mind, she answered him...

Ever hear of a microwave, asshole?

"*Asshole?*" He shouted back at her, yet she knew full and well that she hadn't said a word out loud. "How about if I put your goddamn head in that microwave!"

He lunged at her, and Ian was burly, built like a wall, but she was not the type of woman to be intimidated. Her own temper fueled from the full-force slap; she kicked him in the groin then smashed the side of his face with the glass sugar-bowl she'd snatched from the counter, gashing a slice in the side of his head.

This was the beginning, when the hidden demon inside of Ian had reared its ugly head. The shouting, the cursing, the expletives had continued that night, and through it all, one thing continued to flash in her mind like a beacon shining a warning...

She hadn't said *anything* aloud about the microwave. He had read her thoughts without realizing he had. A sick feeling swept through her that she'd fought with the devil.

And the next morning, regrets, sorrow, and hollow apologies followed. That night had created a distance between them forever. He was changing. Something was happening to him, and yet simultaneously, something was happening to her love for him; it was fading, and somehow he was shamefully aware of this.

But his drinking must have been some early, hidden part of his life because surely it had resurrected. The next night would wipe the day's slate clean, but the irritated sore was left to fester for another time. And many more times there would be.

Ryan would hear them fighting and go back to sleep, but in the morning, he still loved his father. Children could be so resilient, she thought, oblivious to the wrongs parents sometimes commit because they are blind to them in the first place. She was thankful for this, as it maintained some cause for neutrality between them.

She had decided it was time to leave him. How many times could she cover the bruises on her face with makeup? How long would it be before Ryan developed a better understanding of what had really been going on? She had to shield him, deciding that she and her son would move to her Mother's house in a neighboring town.

She sat in the living room, contemplating it all, when the phone rang.

The first sound she heard on the other end was his breathing, rising in the hard, fast panting of a mad, rabid dog. She could identify the slightest sound of him.

"So, you think you're going to just take my kid and leave me? I don't think so, bitch! Do you think I won't find you? Don't make me have to find you!"

The phone was slammed in her ear, silencing the random chatty voices and empty clinking glasses in the background. He was reading her mind, even from where he sat at the bar three blocks away. She broke into tears thinking of all the continuous excuses she had made for him, and now all of the angst and anger within her had turned to sheer terror.

They began to lead separate, non-existent lives. They rarely spoke and barely looked at each other, but the violence dissipated as the fighting soon became random. She took to sleeping in Ryan's room, and the fact that he had suddenly been having nightmares served as a perfect justification.

And then she found the drugs.

The rolled up twenty-dollar bill alongside the line of white powder on the bathroom counter caught her eye. It had been a shock seeing it for the first time in her life. She had never been exposed to it, not even in high school, but she could see exactly what it was. She stood for seconds in stunned silence, feeling the simultaneous dread, contempt, and most of all, disappointment.

She snatched the rolled-up cash from the countertop, and then paced into the living room where he lazed around on the couch watching reruns. The twenty flew in his face by the fast, angry flash of her hand.

"So this is what you're into now? I guess this is where all of our money's been going, right?" She steamed as she continued to pace, waiting for a fight, but he'd said nothing. He didn't move from his position; he just stared at her with the mean arch of his sage-green eyes that now seemed lifeless, vacated of what once lay behind them. The twenty-dollar bill lay untouched on his chest, which moved up and down to the rhythm of his strange but steady breathing. He refocused his odd stare back toward the television.

Strangely, she became alarmed at the fact that he'd made no move toward her. The confusion made her eyes widen in a watchful, glowering glare back at him. She kept her eyes on him as she slowly stepped away from the couch.

"By the way, you left your cocaine on the bathroom counter."

Again, he'd said nothing. She left to pick Ryan up at school.

The next day when she'd taken Ryan back to school and Ian had been at work, she made a secret trip to the local library. She knew there was a name for people who could read minds, but she was unsure what it was, never having paid any attention to such matters in what used to be her normal life. She didn't even believe in that sort of thing, until she'd actually experienced it. Whatever it was, was evil, a capability of that kind could never bring about any good. She had been kept a virtual prisoner because of it.

In fact, she couldn't be sure that Ian wasn't capable of knowing where she was, right this second...could he? Did this thing that he possessed reach that far? If it did, she was silently prepared for it. When she picked Ryan up, she would bring him to a friend's house.

One of the librarians showed her how to research topics using their extensively updated library search engines. She typed in the words "mind reading" and found the word that described the warden of her prison: telepathy.

Most of what she'd read described everything that Ian had demonstrated. He was a telepath, and from what she'd researched, an extremely powerful one. She wondered if Ian even understood what he possessed, but he must have on some level. If he did know, how long had this been part of him; was this what had changed him? She'd read that telepathic abilities begin in early childhood for some, while others develop it in adulthood as either a result of trauma to the brain, or manifesting itself after lying dormant for years.

This would become the secret she would hide from her son about his father.

Their finances had dwindled even further, and Ian began getting strange phone calls at all hours. A friend who frequented the same bar told her the rumors about Ian's increasing cocaine use, and that he'd been getting drugs spotted to him, paying later, and rousing up anger and attention toward himself.

Little did she know that Ian had owed up to fifteen-hundred dollars as a result of his drug habit. It would explain why he was becoming antsy, irritated; she had assumed it was the cocaine. Drug dealers were lurking over him, calling and hounding him for their money. She silently plotted a way to get Ryan out of this house; they would both just have to disappear—damn the consequences for her. She had to protect her son.

After picking Ryan up from his friend's house, she'd brought him home and locked the doors. They had a quiet evening together, as Ian was out again and likely to stay out. She secretly decided that, tomorrow, she would drive her son away from here. There became no question of it when that night she answered the phone.

"*Is Ian there?*" An angry male voice on the other end shouted at her.

"No, he isn't," she said, composing herself, trying to avoid the caller's anger.

"That's okay, I'll find him."

Then, the caller hung up.

It was later that night when she was awakened by Ryan's tortured screams as he reeled in bed from the nightmare of his father, and a few hours after getting him back to sleep, she was roused again by a hard, persistent knocking at the front door. She was sure it was someone for Ian, some irate dealer about to shout a drunken rant at her or even threaten her and Ryan. She would peep through the lace curtains of the front-door window; if she didn't recognize the person, she was calling the police.

Yet it was the police; Ian was dead and an incident over drugs was suspected.

She hadn't told them about the angry caller earlier, because the strange irony of it had swept over her like a cool breeze. Whoever the caller had been, if he was responsible for Ian's death, had removed her burden forever, setting her free. She felt an almost unspeakable debt of gratitude and a bizarre sense of allegiance to this dark and anonymous pardoner.

She told them she didn't know whom Ian was dealing with, nor did she discover his cocaine use until recently, all of which was the truth. She sat stunned by the fact that her son had just dreamed the reality she was now listening to, and of course, she'd made no mention of this to the police either.

But now she would have a deeply bereaved and possibly traumatized child on her hands. How was she supposed to tell him that his nightmare had come true? Ryan adored his Dad, and though Ian was a son-of-a-bitch, he was ultimately a good father. He wasn't always drunken and abusive, the way he'd been toward the end, not for the first couple of years she'd known him. She would never know what had completely changed him, but she would mourn for the person Ian once was. Ryan continued to hear the voice of his father. She didn't believe any of it at first, figuring that Ryan was grieving and trying to hold on to Ian any way he knew how, but then he told her things that only Ian would know. Then, the other voices came, and many of Ryan's predictions had come true, all because "the voices had told him."

The fear of what was happening to her son was a constant, blaring alarm she could not shut down. The freedom from the life with Ian she'd felt after his death was fleeting in the face of the fact that he'd passed his strange psychic bloodline down to their son. Soon after, Sidney Pratt had pronounced Ryan as a clairaudient; Ryan was able to hear the voices of the dead, as well as remotely perceive the conversations of living people. Fear and devastation had swept over her.

She had never mentioned Ian's telepathy to Ryan, or to the investigators, fearing they would make a freak of her son, study him under a microscope to learn the extent of his capabilities, and make him their latest "discovery." Sidney had never said anything about Ryan being able to read minds—maybe he would never develop his father's ability. She would just stay silent and pray, pray that it would leave him.

Her feat of keeping Ryan away from the investigators had finally failed. Ryan was now headed to the hospital; he was hell-bent on seeing

Sidney. She felt a slight twinge inside of her, a sickly omen telling her that the secret she'd tried to keep was slowly slipping away. She knew she couldn't hold out much longer; everything was coming unraveled.

The hospital's heliport loomed closely into her view. She was only three blocks away from the coming confrontation, and her raw nerves jittered in a flurry.

Chapter Six

The immaculate white rolled away like a fog, unveiling the brilliance of a bright, beautiful, summer day. Above him, the sky stretched magnificently, an unblemished baby-blue blanket being warmed by the blinding sun. Before him, a familiar river oddly rippled with a clean, crystalline blue that competed with the perfect sky, and the dock where he and Grandpa had fished shined a perfect painted white beneath the sun. He was enraptured by the temporal utopia, euphoric in of itself, magnificent in its appearance.

He stepped onto the dock, and out of nowhere, a man began walking toward him. His heart nearly leapt from his chest as he recognized him; it was Grandpa, yet the old man's appearance was somehow different. He was sharper, more refined, his face tightened and unwrinkled and sporting a youthful glow.

Soon, they stood face to face, with Sidney's mouth upturned in a nervous and tearful outcry of joy as Grandpa smiled in unsurprised reassurance.

"Hello, Sidney, my boy," he said, his strong voice seeming to echo through the expanse of boundless time. Sidney struggled to speak from the wincing pain in his throat.

"Grandpa, am I dead?"

The old man closed his lips and sighed.

"No, Sidney, you're not dead. You're here, but you're not dead."

"Then why am I here? What's happening?" His state of confusion intensified.

"I'm afraid you had a close call, Sidney, but now is not your time."

"But I want to stay, with you, and this place, it's—"

"You can't, Sidney. You will go back, after you've finished your journey."

"Journey?"

"It happens in life to many people," he said to him, gazing straight into his eyes. "There are things you need to figure out, Sidney. I can't give you the answers; you need to find those out for yourself. Only you can do that."

"What answers?"

"About your life, Sidney, about this thing you've carried around for most of it. It's essential that you understand."

"But, I do understand, I—"

"Not everything, Sidney. How could you at such a young age." He smiled and admired his grandson once again, who stood before him now beneath the brilliant light as a grown man. "You will learn everything you need to, Sidney, and then you will go back, where you will be needed."

"But, Grandpa, wait!" He heard his own cries, and they were somehow greater in timbre. Then the old man smiled and blended with the light.

Suddenly, the scene changed; the river and the dock disappeared in a flash and were instantly replaced by another setting. He found himself standing in the front yard of the family home, where he had lived with his parents and Grandpa; its white vinyl siding and black shutters were exactly as he remembered it. How could this be? The atmosphere around him seemed undeniable as the constant chirping of birds intermingled with the soft, rustling breeze that swept through the trees, and even the aroma of freshly mowed grass hung thickly in the air.

Yet underneath those various sounds came a soft, quiet sobbing that came from the front porch. He moved his eyes in that direction and caught sight of a little boy. He moved a few steps closer for a better glance, but he recognized the boy in an instant—it was himself at age five.

An inner instinct also recognized this particular moment in time, and the occurrence that followed was just as he expected. The shroud of deafness had descended over everything, silencing the birds, the rustling leaves, and the young, sobbing Sidney. The deafness had enveloped him even in this strange utopia, and Grandpa's voice called out again.

"Sidney! Search from here Sidney...do you remember what I said to you that day?" Then the moment replayed itself, as if to remind him.

"I love you, Sidney, always."

He watched as the boy that he once was raised his head upward to the sky in disbelief at the voice, shock at the deafness, the eyes rolling slightly upward, the chest heaving faster.

A genuine tear rolled down his cheek.

"I know, Grandpa," he called out.

"I chose to speak to you, Sidney, because I knew you could hear me. This is where it all began. Search through time, Sidney, from this moment on."

The sounds returned in full clarity.

The boy roused with a start from the porch and ran into the house, calling out for Mom and Dad in a child's voice that once was his own. Sidney moved quickly, swinging the front door open and entering, as though it were nothing, and followed the boy into the house.

"Mom, Dad, Mom, Dad!" The sound of his once puerile voice, becoming more and more familiar, had unlocked forgotten memories of his childhood, as well as the sight of the house the way it was years ago: the green living room carpet, the white wallpaper that covered the walls above the staircase, the chipped wooden banister he'd slid down every morning before breakfast.

Knowing that the boy was headed for the kitchen, he followed fast behind him, and then suddenly stopped where he stood. The memory of this moment had returned in full detail, and the sequence of events burst through an unlocked door in his mind. He stood and stared at the running child and the kitchen doors that he knew would open—and they did.

The double doors flew open, and he watched as the younger figures of Mom and Dad stepped out. The child grabbed onto and held the hem of his mother's dress, and his father knelt down before him, clutching and combing him to make sure he was all right.

"Mom, Dad, Grandpa's still here. He's still here! I heard him...outside!"

"What do you mean, you heard him?" Sidney now recognized that the exaggerated tone of disbelief in his father's voice was meant for someone else; they had company, the Fullers, the two neighbors that stood behind his parents in the frame of the double doors. As they'd come out to see what was happening, the child stepped slightly away, made to feel embarrassed.

"I couldn't hear anything, and then I heard Grandpa's voice. I did, I did hear him!"

His mother's lips parted in pristine astonishment. Her eyes opened wide as the child's ramblings made her nervous at first, and then mortified. His father's eyes closed in equal embarrassment. The child looked up at the neighbors, and even now, Sidney recalled that look with photographic recollection, the wide-eyed look of fear and misunderstanding.

"Son, what did I tell you about the wild imagination, huh? Now, you only imagined you heard Grandpa, and you know that. You wanted to hear him, so you did."

"Sidney, we thought you were hurt! You scared the daylights out of us!" His mother clasped her chest, a purely dramatic effect for her guests, whom she turned to. "Sidney's been having a hard time with Michael's father's death." She shook her head, letting out a final gasp, as young Sidney continued his unacknowledged protests.

It had been the Fullers who had first suggested a psychiatrist.

Now, the brilliant white overwhelmed everything in its path with a blinding iridescence that soon faded away, unveiling yet another scenario. He found himself seated next to his younger self in the backseat of Dad's Chevy that through the years, he'd forgotten. Dad was driving and Mom rode shotgun, while he rode in the back, playing with the Rubik's cube Grandpa had bought him.

He was a little older than the last scenario he'd witnessed, probably eight or nine. What was so important about this particular car ride with his parents? It had been one of many; yet simultaneously, it also seemed familiar.

The child sat turning the tiers of the colored cube to the right, and to the left, oblivious to his parents' front seat discussion. But now with this strange gift of returned time, Sidney was able to hear what he'd missed, misunderstood, or simply ignored. He gazed out the window while he listened, watching winter's bare trees pass one after another out of sight.

"What do you think is going to make this shrink any different? You think she is going to say something that the rest of them haven't?" His father's voice was pressing toward his mother, yet it remained calm, subdued in censorship because of the child in the backseat.

"It's worth a shot, Michael," his mother said, quietly. "There is more to this than what we originally thought."

"I thought we were in agreement that this was all part of his overactive imagination? That's what the other doctors said."

"We *were* in agreement, Michael. That was before he started mentioning people he would have no way of knowing about."

"Come on, Cindy. We had to have mentioned those people at sometime—"

"No, we did not! I want to know how, and why, he is able to know or hear certain things, and these doctors haven't given us anything that satisfies me."

They had been talking about the time when he'd mentioned hearing one of their high-school friends who had passed on, as well as a distant cousin. He also spoke out on things that only Mom and Dad would've known, like the miscarriage his mother suffered before his birth. They had never told Sidney he would have had an older sibling, but he knew, and it disturbed his mother.

The elder Sidney saw his father's quick glance into the backseat to make sure the child had been occupied.

"Maybe he's just a whack job, like your brother."

"Michael! I don't want you saying things like that in front of him, or her, for that matter. She is a highly esteemed psychiatrist; she will blame the whole thing on us."

Now, Sidney remembered. He recalled hearing that last part of the conversation long ago, but he hadn't understood. Why would the doctor blame Mom and Dad? He'd asked himself that question at the time, and the answer was much clearer now. This was the day they'd taken him to see the esteemed female psychiatrist—Dr. Susan Logan.

* * * *

They'd been sitting in her office when he'd met her the first time. She'd been in her forties then, youthful in appearance, blond hair and blue eyes, and a friendly, feminine voice. She had asked Sidney various questions: how he liked school, his friends, and the time he spent with Grandpa; she asked what he wanted to be. Then she asked about the voices.

He told her about the time he'd first heard his grandfather, and about the deafness, how he couldn't hear anything else when it happened. Some fleeting, changing expression on her face silently told Sidney that he'd broken through to her, that possibly, Dr. Logan might believe him.

She'd ordered more sessions with him, and now, as he watched each one of them over again, they strangely seemed part of the same sequence, as though they were all one occasion. His parents had mentioned a word to her that he did not understand—schizophrenic. But he understood enough to know that it had something to do with hearing voices that weren't there. The voices he'd heard were there, and he could prove it.

"I sincerely doubt that," Dr. Logan had said. "That condition is extremely rare in children, and besides, Sidney lacks all of the other symptoms; he is otherwise a perfectly well-behaved, rational, happy boy. There is a joyful contentment inside Sidney that is not present in those with the condition you just mentioned, but I still want to go a little further with him."

The collage of sequenced events mixed together and soon, Susan Logan was trying to retrieve from him a confession through an aggressive, verbal onslaught. Susan had later told him she'd been testing his sincerity under pressure.

"Did you really hear your Grandfather, Sidney? Tell us, really? Couldn't it have been all in your mind? It was wasn't it? You heard what you wanted to hear, Sidney, and you exaggerated the rest. Am I right? Tell us!"

"No," he'd said, confidently.

"You know what they say about people who say such things, don't you, Sidney? Now, tell me the truth. This is upsetting your parents to no end—"

That was the moment where she continued to speak, but no sound came from her mouth, as he looked her straight in the face. He heard sounds of gunfire, like the war movies Grandpa had watched on TV, and then a man's voice spoke...

"Call her Suzy Q, and tell her Mark loves her."

The deafness died away, and the older Sidney watched for the reaction on Susan Logan's face for the second time in history, knowing what the child would reveal to her.

"Sidney, what's wrong?" She asked the child.

"Mark says he loves you, Suzy Q."

Her reaction was exactly as he remembered it: her face dropping and draining of color, the paleness overshadowing her rouge, and big blue eyes widening as her mouth opened in a speechless stupor. He turned in time to catch a similar expression on his mother's face, which bore the perfect combination of fright and ignorance. And then Mom and Dad's eyes had met, locking in terror, confusion.

He remembered the long silence that had followed this revelation, edgy and unnerving, filling the room. For just a moment his focus strayed from the visions as something twinged inside of him after hearing Mark's voice a second time. The voice, like everything else in this odd state of being, was familiar—closely familiar. But then again, he had heard the voice many years ago, and it seemed as though it had never left him. It was also different somehow, just like the boy, not one of the dead, but how could that be?

Susan's voice broke the stringent silence in the recreation of that moment.

"Mr. and Mrs. Pratt, may I see you for a moment, outside?"

The scene changed again to a one-on-one session with Susan, without his parents, and just the two of them sat in her office.

"What do you know about him, Sidney? Tell me."

"Nothing," he'd said. "I just heard gunfire, you know, like in war movies, and he talked to me. He said he loves you, and he told me to call you, 'Suzy Q.'"

Her eyebrows rose upward, expressing the pointed painful arch of a broken, bleeding heart. An unconscious murmur muttered beneath her breath.

"So, he *is* dead?" She caught herself and looked up at her young patient. "Can you speak with him now, Sidney? What else did he tell you?" Her questions became incessant, and even now, he could still see that determined, obsessed look in her blue eyes.

In an instant flash, he was back inside the house, and his parents were arguing.

"I'm telling you, I don't like her!" His father yelled at his mother, whose demeanor was still clearly shaken by the episode in Susan's office. Sidney could see her hands quivering, and the watchful look of fear hadn't left her eyes.

"Michael, I'm scared. I'm terrified of whatever this is. Whatever this ability our son has, I want it gone!" His mother clutched both hands together, the way she always did, silently praying her wishes to prevail.

"I'm not so sure I want to know," his father said. "And besides, do you think she is going to label him as 'gifted?' Hell no! She will make a project out of our son, and soon enough, she will call him crazy! Is that what you want, Cindy? Is it? Like it isn't bad enough that people are already talking!"

She had started to cry, her hand reaching for her forehead in hopelessness.

"Listen, maybe this thing will go away. We will take him to church with us, Cindy. It's how we were raised. 'Ask and ye shall receive,' it says, and that's what we'll do. We will just pray that God takes this thing away from him." He pulled her toward him, clutching and holding her, his voice reassuring, but unconvinced himself.

And then the memories of attending church with them passed in a series of various images like a slideshow. He enjoyed going to church; he'd always felt safe there, comforted. Mom and Dad hadn't mentioned his ability for a while during this time; they just kept silent, cautious that he had said no more about it and grateful that he was attending church with them.

The next vision showed him at the age of sixteen, when he'd finally revealed to his parents that he was still hearing his grandfather—and others. That was when all of the lively dinner conversations, the family fun, the hugs, the warmth, the compromise, had all died away. Michael and Cindy's son was not what they had dreamed and hoped, and their prayers for his detestable talent to dissipate had fallen on divinely deaf ears. This thing that possessed him was not right; they wanted no part of it, and so they'd erected a wall of silence between them and their son.

He saw visions of these years where he'd studied hard, day and night, acing exams one right after another. Then came the day in his senior year when he was notified of his full-scholarship acceptance at the university; at last, he would be out of this house, free of parents who treated him as an outsider and a freak with their continued silence.

They did help him move from the house to his dorm, and that day he could almost feel the relief that exuded from them. They were free to live their lives without fear and embarrassment, yet Sidney was free to explore who he really was and be able to understand this thing from a rational, academic standpoint.

He excelled at the university, as expected, and soon learned of the paranormal investigative society that had made quite a reputable name for itself through its research and progress in paranormal investigations. What would they think of him? Would they understand what he was, or were they a bunch of ghost groupies, wasting valuable time on fruitless expeditions, jumping at every sound they heard, and attributing such noises to the dead? The solid reputation that preceded them certainly didn't correspond to that idea.

Still, he would try not to shock them.

He watched himself apprehensively knocking on the door of Room 208; it was the first time he had met Dylan Rasche and Brett Taylor. After a voice had bid him entry, he opened the heavy door and found the two young men seated around one of the television screens, viewing a video. They had been heavy in conversation and light in laughter, of which he'd awkwardly interrupted.

"Hi, is this the paranormal investigative society?" His voice sounded low, timid.

The tall young man with the curly, black hair, slightly older than himself, stood up from his chair to greet him.

"Yes. Hello, I'm Dylan Rasche," he'd said, shaking his hand. "Is there something I can help you with?"

"I'm Sidney Pratt. I'm a newly arrived freshman...and...Well, I was kind of interested in your group." Sidney felt the need to get to know them first before springing his ability on them. If they were phonies, the last thing he needed was the attention, the whole campus regarding him as a rarity, and life continuing much as it had at home.

He looked around the room as he said this, seeing the vast array of technical apparatus: televisions, computers, video cameras, and devices he had never seen before.

All of it looked expensive, high-tech, and something assured him that this assortment of costly equipment belonged only to serious ghost hunters.

The other young man with the long, shoulder-length hair and green army jacket also stood to greet him.

"I'm Brett Taylor," he said, also shaking Sidney's hand.

"Well, welcome, Sidney," Dylan continued. "Now that you've met both of us, please have a seat. Let us tell you what we're about."

"So is it just you two guys?" Sidney asked, having glanced around the room, not seeing anyone else.

"Well, no," Brett said. "Sometimes we have classes that study with us, some people have come and gone, and sometimes we have volunteers and researchers, but it is the two of us who run and maintain this little operation."

"There is also a board of directors that sponsors our society," Dylan added. "They rarely intervene with our investigations; we just keep them posted on our research, progress, etc. So tell me, Sidney, what brings you here? Have you ever had any paranormal experiences? It's usually personal experience that brings interested parties to us. What is it for you, Sidney?"

There it was and so early. He wished he could have waited, but they asked. He thought of the best way to begin, the most articulate way to describe, when unexpectedly, the deafness overcame him. He knew what was happening, and his mouth must have dropped because the two young men sat up further in their chairs and stared at him.

And one of the unknown dead spoke...

"The young man who needs a haircut calls me Aunt Viv— you can too. Tell him I'm watching. Tell him to take care of Uncle Jack."

She'd sounded content, almost enlightened. His ears had popped as they usually did when his hearing returned. He looked at them, especially Brett; the concern on their faces revealed that they had noticed something.

It was now or never. He took a deep breath while continuing to stare at Brett, who instinctively drew closer to him. Then Sidney let him have it...

"Your Aunt Viv says to get your hair cut."

Brett's face blanched a sickly pale, and his brown eyes stared endlessly in shock. Physically, his upper body bucked backward, as if the astonishment had dealt a blow to his chest. He looked at Dylan, then back at Sidney, who continued.

"She says to make sure you take care of Uncle Jack for her."

Brett hung his head down with a gasp and tightened his eyes shut, forcing back the forging painful tears that threatened his already bewildered demeanor. He looked back at Dylan again, who'd kept his eyes on Sidney as he spoke.

"He's a clairaudient."

It was the first time Sidney had ever heard the word.

Brett explained that his Aunt Vivian and Uncle Jack had raised him after being given up by his teenage mother, who was unable to care for him at such a young age. Aunt Viv and Uncle Jack, the only parents he'd ever known, had adopted him. Aunt Vivian had died five years ago of heart failure.

"She says she's watching you." Sidney had tried to sound consoling, reassuring.

"Sidney, how long have you had this ability?" Dylan asked, as his eyes locked in fascination at the marvel that had walked through the door.

"I first noticed it after my grandfather died; I was only five at the time."

In this vision, he had been an eighteen-year-old college freshman, and he watched as his younger self explained the details that had followed his grandfather's death, comfortable that they would understand. The looks on their faces were attentive, absorbed, almost infatuated, and he'd sat back in unspoken relief.

"You called me something a minute ago," Sidney said to Dylan. "What was it?"

"A clairaudient," Dylan said. "I assume you are unaware of what that means?"

Sidney shrugged his shoulders; Dylan continued...

"Clairaudients are individuals who can hear the voices of the dead. I'm sure you're aware of that much."

Sidney was stunned by this confirmation, but still, he nodded.

"Much like clairvoyants can see the future, and some see the dead, clairaudients can hear the dead speak. Often spirits are aware that the clairaudient, or the listener, can hear them; something about that person attracts them so they speak, knowing the listener will hear them."

Dylan spoke with an apparent wealth of paranormal knowledge and experience, but still, Sidney felt the need to explain.

"But sometimes, I don't always hear a spirit as strongly as I can hear my grandfather, or as clearly as I heard Brett's aunt. Sometimes, there are only words or broken sentences, and sometimes the voices overlap, and it's hard to hear exactly what they're saying."

"Yes," Dylan said. "That is because that particular spirit is not strong enough to communicate as well as others. Usually, clairaudients hear the voices of loved ones more precisely, even random spirits if the person meant for the message is present, as Brett was. The overlapping voices occur when several spirits communicate simultaneously.

"Some clairaudients even possess a stronger ability than that; some can hear the voices of the living from other locations, sometimes miles away, a feat called 'remote hearing.' Often, clairaudients are misdiagnosed as schizophrenics. Your ability, Sidney, is a form of telepathy, though not manifested in the mind-reading sense.

The elder Sidney watched and remembered how his mind was reeling from the clarification of what he was, and what he wasn't. He'd felt vindicated. Susan Logan had been right; he wasn't crazy, but something about that conclusion made the situation somewhat darker.

"Sidney, what you have is a rare gift, though not unheard of. Those who are able to hear the dead are mentioned as far back as the Bible. As I said, there are people in the world that can see the dead, and there are some that can hear them; they are individuals with an authentic, psychic gift that the world has not yet come to understand."

He remembered being caught off-guard by the biblical mention and wishing his parents would have been there to hear it. How he longed to see the expressions that would've appeared on their faces. Had his parents known all along about clairaudients, given the biblical mention? Was that why they had stopped him from seeing Susan? He continued to watch the younger renditions of himself, Dylan, and Brett, in what had been a day of great revelation and discovery.

He'd gone on to tell them about Susan Logan, though he hadn't mentioned her by name. When they'd asked about his family, he was honest.

"Being an only child can be rough, lonely," Brett volunteered. "I loved Aunt Viv and I love Uncle Jack endlessly, but I know what it's like to be the only child. To live with this ability in addition to that couldn't have been easy. I feel for you, Sidney."

"There are many parents," Dylan said, "who are terrified by their child's psychic ability, who don't understand, who are somehow threatened by it. Unfortunately, those parents often alienate their child out of their fear. Please know in your heart, Sidney, that it's that fear that keeps them from you."

He witnessed the vision change, fast-forwarding through the passing years when he learned everything that Dylan had referenced on clairaudience. He studied for hours in the campus library and sometimes well into the night, reading up on cases around the world. He delved vigorously into the area of child psychics, after all, he'd been one of them, and discovered that most of what had occurred in his childhood was not so unusual.

Within a few years, the three had become close friends and working partners. They brought him on ghost hunting expeditions and locations of hauntings, and many times Sidney was able to hear the spirit, ghost, or the often malignant, unseen presence. He'd studied his ability through his psychic research, engrossing himself in it constantly, until there was nothing left to learn.

He had become an expert, and they had become a trio.

Then one day, a beautiful, petite, young girl had also walked through the door of Room 208. She had been a formidable counterpart in every opposite aspect of the word; she could see the dead. She'd sought out the society because at the young age of nineteen, her experiences had turned her into a paragon of psychic phenomena.

Leah Leeds had also been the age of five when she first began to see spirits. Her parents had lived in an old manor house on Cedar Drive that was not too far from where Sidney had lived, and he knew the house by sight. She told of it having been haunted, and how spirits, ghosts, visions, and poltergeists had tormented her at such a young age. Her mother had died in that house, the same house where her father had left his sanity behind, and the haunting memories continued to plague her as an adult.

Sidney taught her most of what he'd learned about psychic abilities in children, and they researched and studied together. The society had approached Leah with the idea of writing about her experience in that house and composing it into a memoir exclusively published for the society, a task which he'd helped her complete. The final product had been a shocker to all who had read it. Together, they had solved only a small part of the mystery behind that house.

The four of them had become like siblings, and when not undertaking expeditions, they sat quietly dwelling in their close-knit, safe haven, studying, researching, keeping clear and open minds ready for whatever paranormal occurrences awaited their expertise.

Dylan and Brett did not actually possess psychic abilities, but their knowledge and experience was infinite on a grand scale. They were technical wizards, capable of understanding and maintaining the various electromagnetic technologies used to identify paranormal phenomena. They were a scholarly ensemble, yet a motley crew, as Sidney and Leah became perfect fitting pieces to an incomplete puzzle.

Now the young boy that Sidney had seen earlier entered the ever-changing scene. He had been one of Sidney's brief subjects of study; his reddish-brown hair and deep green eyes were vaguely familiar. His inner instinct told him that he was seeing the memory of this boy for a reason; he searched his mind to remember his name. The boy ogled him with a far-away look in his eyes, almost coaxing Sidney to remember, and then he spoke...

"The back roads, Sidney...remember...the back roads."

He recognized the voice, the voice of the boy he'd heard the night of Tracy Kimball's accident. It was *him.* He was the living voice that had told him where to search for Tracy. The boy's name was forming in his mind like a blooming bud on a May morning. Then suddenly, it came to him...

"Ryan!" He shouted out the name he'd so desperately fought to recall. Ryan, it was Ryan. Ryan was the listener. Of course, it made sense now; Ryan could hear the living, as well as the dead! He must have been listening during the search for Tracy, and he was trying to help.

Ryan continued to stare at him with eyes that were strangely and silently pleading. Sidney recalled that Ryan had been brought to the team by his mother. Later, she'd stopped the sessions with them, the same way his parents had with Susan. And as soon as that thought crossed his mind, Ryan was gone.

* * * *

The blinding whiteness surrounded him once again as the various chronological scenes of his life had come to a close like the end of a movie, yet no credits rolled by. Only the thick fog of the whiteness that greeted him early on remained, encircling and engulfing him in a rapturous hold. He looked every which way around him, so difficult to see through the white, yet the outline of something moved toward him.

What was it? In this state of being, he was without his glasses, and he squinted to see what object moved before him. As the outline neared, he realized it was no object—it was a person, coming toward him through the whiteness. He watched as the figure moved gracefully through the fog.

His heart leapt and broke in a combination of joy and sorrow as he recognized the figure that came closer. Her long, brown hair appeared different, feathered, luxurious, while her face was refined, tight, and youthful, devoid of the light wrinkles and sagging eyes that had resulted in life from her vice. Even Tracy Kimball's gray eyes gleamed as she neared him, an angelic smile spread across her beautiful face.

"Hello, Sidney." Her voice was soft and harmonious, rising into the air with a minute echo. She walked right up to him as the tears rolled down his face. Then slowly, she reached out with the same ruffle-sleeved hand he'd touched in the casket, and she took his hand. It was warm and soft, not dead and stone hard the way he remembered. His sobs were now groans that escaped his imprisoned heart, echoing out into the vast everywhere.

"Don't cry, Sidney. It's so good to see you."

He clutched her in a gripping hug, her hair swiftly tickling his cheek. She smelled of lavender. He could feel her; she was real. Then he pulled away to catch a closer look at her face. Her hand reached up and wiped the tears from his eyes.

"Tracy, I'm sorry." He said, trying not to lose it, knowing that their time would be brief. She smiled back at him in wonder.

"Sorry for what, Sidney?"

"I couldn't save you! It was my job to save you, and I failed you! This is my fault!"

Her smile dissipated, as though she scoffed at the sound of stupidity.

"Sidney, it *was not* your fault, nor was it your job to save me. It was *my* job to save me, Sidney. Don't you see, I willingly danced with fate, and it overcame me? I let my addiction get the best of me. You did so much for me, Sid, all of you did."

"But...how?" His voice was adamant, confused.

"You brought me closer to David. You are the one who heard his warnings when it was my job to hear them. I failed to heed the warnings, Sidney, just like Leah said.

"David?" Sidney asked, and Tracy smiled once again, nodding her head. She motioned with her eyes just over her left shoulder. Behind her, another figure moved in toward them, and soon he recognized the face he'd seen in the picture. It was David. His sandy brown hair and muscular form stepped closely behind her, and they stood together, a perfect and eternal couple.

"Hello, Sidney," he said, his arms encompassing his eternal bride. "Thank you."

Again, he protested with a tremor in his voice.

"Sidney, don't you see," Tracy said. "I would have been damned by my own actions, but you brought me closer to David, and because you did, I am not. I am here, and he is here with me."

In a way, Sidney understood, but in another way, he didn't. There wasn't time to debate; his time was slipping away fast once again, just like the ghostly hourglass he'd raced to beat trying to save her.

"Sidney, I am fine," she said. "Unfortunately, you are not; that's why you're here. There isn't much time left, Sidney...listen."

She motioned as he moved in even closer toward her, and she continued.

"It's Ryan, Sidney. You have to help Ryan; he's in danger. Now that you remember him, you have to wake up, and you have to help him."

"In danger from what?"

"Not from what, Sidney, from whom. You must hurry. I can't tell you anymore, but Sidney, you were right about voices being familiar during this journey. You were right, Sidney. Remember the voice—the one you know you've heard before."

He tried to think back on the order of the visions he'd experienced.

"It's about that time, buddy. Take care, until we meet again sometime." David touched his shoulder when he spoke—so real.

"Take care, my friend," Tracy said, clutching her arms around him once again. "We will see each other again, I promise you."

He held onto her, crying, and then they were gone. The whiteness was clearing, being sucked away by the shifting of time. As it cleared, he could see the corridor once more. His movements were less weighted now, light as though he were gliding. The odd ultra-violet sun was nowhere to be found as he made his way through the corridor, searching for his way out.

* * * *

Dr. Greg Talbot had stitched the final sutures in Sidney Pratt's head; he would awaken—hopefully soon. He remained stable, enduring the surgery as though he were in some dream-filled sleep state. Again, Talbot wondered what dreams and thoughts manifested inside the unconscious mind of a patient. Whatever it was for Sidney Pratt, it had helped him through.

"That's it," he said. "Get him into recovery. When he wakes, we'll know more about whether the surgery was a success. He should be fine and fully functional."

Talbot made his way to the scrub room, his hands held upward in the air. He would scrub, and then relay the news to Susan Logan that Sidney Pratt was going to make it.

Chapter Seven

They'd sat in the hospital lounge for over three hours, fearing, worrying, and silently praying. No one had told them anything about Sidney yet, so Brett and Dylan went to the hospitality shop to bring back food while they waited. Leah and Susan were now alone, giving them both a chance to discuss the disturbing visions that had been haunting Leah as of late. They sat comfortably inside, a warm relief from the cold October rain outside.

"Leah, let's start from where the visions began." Susan automatically assumed the role of the highly effective psychiatrist that she was. Since the tragedy of Tracy Kimball, the hospital had discovered that Susan had long ago achieved yet another degree, one in Parapsychology. This fact she'd kept hidden out of fear of being the subject of ridicule, discredited, or even shunned. The hospital had no complaints, as they were not willing to lose their highly effective psychiatrist to another hospital.

"The visions started right around the time that Tracy came to see us," she said, her voice searching for the finest details inside her mind.

"After Tracy met you all?" Susan asked, exploring the possibility of a connection to Tracy.

"No, it started a little bit before that. I was seeing it all again when I was telling her about that time in my life. It was strange because that's rarely happened to me since writing the memoir."

"You mean you were seeing the things that happened, in your mind, all over again? Well, that is normal isn't it?" Susan tried the logical approach first.

"No, I wasn't seeing in my mind, or with my mind. I saw with my eye, my third eye. I saw the events happening again, in vision form."

Susan had known all about "third eye" and knew that Leah Leeds had possessed an eminently powerful one, but it was the first time she'd ever heard her use the phrase.

"Tell me what you saw, Leah." Her voice was soft, coaxing in the cozy lounge.

"Lately, I've been seeing my mother. She hung herself in that house, and I keep seeing her hanging from the balcony, the noose around her neck, her body swinging, and her feet swaying beneath her skirt from above."

"But, you didn't see that, am I right?" Susan knew the details of that house from treating Leah's father, Paul, after the ordeal. She had also seen the police photos; Leah's description was exact, like hitting a bull's-eye with one hand.

"I didn't see it then, no. But, I think I have now."

"You mean you're seeing with your third eye what you had been fortunate enough, at the time, not to see?"

Leah's lips spread in an ironic smile across her face, as if an ancient wisdom made the young seer certain of the answer. She closed her eyes and nodded affirmatively.

"What do you think is causing you to see these things from the past with your third eye?" A thoughtful, unbroken silence passed between them as Leah thought, searching for a response.

"I can't be sure, but whatever it is has to do with that house. I can feel it."

Their unofficial session was abruptly interrupted by the slight squeak of the door as it swung open, and Dylan and Brett entered with pizza from the hospitality shop. Susan quickly changed the subject, and Leah showed no sign of her mounting distress. They sat eating and talking until a nurse entered the lounge. They stood to hear the news.

"Please sit, no worries," she said. "Dr. Talbot has informed me to tell you that Sidney Pratt is out of surgery."

"And?" Susan asked, approaching the nurse.

"He is optimistic that Sidney should be fine as soon as he wakes up, but he's not out of the woods, yet. The sooner he wakes the better. The surgery was an overall success."

Susan's face dropped in relief as gasps of bottled tension expelled in unison.

"Dr. Talbot said he will be in to see you, soon, Dr. Logan."

Susan thanked her as she left, and the four of them embraced at answered prayers.

* * * *

The sounds of their voices rose higher in pitch, ringing out through the hospital lounge, celebratory of the fact that they were not faced with yet another tragedy. But when the nurse returned within minutes, the celebration was cut with a sharp apprehension. The slight squint of her eyes displayed concern and confusion.

"I'm sorry to interrupt, but there is a young boy here, insisting to see Sidney Pratt. He says he's a friend. I told him he couldn't see Sidney, right now, so he's asked to see Dylan."

"A young boy?" Dylan asked.

"He said you would know him."

Dylan told her to show him in, and after stepping out, she returned with the boy. The investigators recognized him immediately by his reddish-brown hair and deep green eyes.

"Ryan! So good to see you, my friend. How did you get here?" Dylan asked, his tone skeptical, knowing the answer wouldn't be good.

"I walked," he said. "I'm here to see Sidney. Is he okay?"

"Sidney is going to be fine." Susan stepped forward; the inquisitive look on her face wanted to know just who this boy was. "He is out of surgery, but we can't see him just yet. I'm Dr. Logan; I'm Sidney's friend also. Ryan, is it?"

He nodded his head and continued.

"I need to see Sidney, fast, as soon as he wakes up." The urgency in his voice commanded their attention.

"Does your mother know you're here?" Leah asked, her eyes motioning to the rest of the team.

"No, I snuck out, but I'm sure she knows I'm gone by now."

Dylan sighed, lifted his eyes, and lowered his head.

"Okay, so, Ryan, you want to tell me what was so important that you would sneak out of the house and walk all the way across town to come here?"

"I heard something, and you have to help me. There is a man coming to kidnap me because he couldn't use Sidney for what he wanted. He knows about me because he listens, like I do." Ryan's words rolled off in a flurry, becoming so much information in so little time.

"Okay, okay," Dylan said, surprised, yet calming him. "Slow down,

Ryan; I need you to think, and then tell me exactly what you heard."

Dylan and the others knew the extent of Ryan's capabilities; however, Susan was unacquainted with the fact that the young boy's abilities far outweighed even Sidney's. Still, she watched in silent fascination.

Ryan told them about hearing the man's voice, about overhearing the phone conversation, and learning how the man had been stalking Sidney for years because he was also a listener. He told how the man mentioned his name, knowing about him because he was once a study subject of Sidney's, saying that "the kid" was a more powerful listener. He needed Ryan for some secret project, and he was going to kidnap him.

"When did you hear all of this?" Dylan asked.

"I've been hearing things about Sidney for a few days now, ever since that girl was in the accident, but I started to hear this man today. I even remember his name."

"What was his name?" Dylan didn't think there would be any relevance to knowing this mysterious man's name, but if Ryan heard something that concerned Sidney, and if Ryan was in danger because of it, it was best that the team knew all that he had heard.

"Hadley—his name was Hadley."

The look on Ryan's face when he heard the astonishment erupt in the room was as though he'd said something wrong. Leah and Brett rose from the table and hurried forward, and Susan moved in a little closer to the boy.

"Hadley?" Leah asked. "*Roman* Hadley?" The sound of incredulity in her voice spoke on behalf of the entire team.

The impact of hearing Ryan name their unseen, anonymous society head caused the team to feel the substantial shock in unison. Ryan could not have made up this assertion because he had no idea who Roman Hadley was. They had never even met Roman Hadley; their contact with him had consisted of telephone conversations. Even Susan, newly inducted onto the board of directors, had only heard the name mentioned.

If what Ryan was saying was true, then Hadley was using them, watching them, stalking his main interest, Sidney Pratt, from afar. There would be a connection if Hadley was a listener himself as Ryan claimed.

"I never heard his first name, but he's coming to get me! He can't get to Sidney, and he said something about Sidney not being able to hear the living."

"Okay, Ryan," Brett said, taking the boy aside. "Now, you know that we're not going to let anything happen to you, right? You're safe here with us; you're in a hospital."

Dylan became speechless, and for the first time, unaware of how to handle the situation. He turned and looked at Susan, his expression pleading for help.

"Ryan," Susan said, "Why don't you come over here, and sit with us at the table? It will give you a chance to calm down, and we can talk about this some more." She enticed him with pizza, and he repeated everything he remembered hearing, exactly as he'd heard it. Then Dylan explained to Susan who Ryan was, and that he was a listener once studied by Sidney.

Then the swing of the door interrupted them again, and this time, the nurse brought with her, Annie, Ryan's mother. Her big brown eyes stared straight at her son, and the irate expression on her face was equally direct. Her lips were pulled tight, rapid breathing quelling rising anger just underneath. She stared at him, and then looked at them, as though they were the apparent causes.

"Ryan Quinn! What do you think you're doing?"

* * * *

"So, you mean to tell me that my son is a target because of his psychic ability and now in danger of being kidnapped?" Annie voiced the sounds of hostility and frustration as they explained to her what had taken place just before she arrived.

Susan took control of the situation, first by introducing herself as who she was to the team, and then as a psychiatrist at the hospital. She convinced everyone to be seated around the table in the lounge to discuss the situation, and listen, for Ryan's sake. Then, she instructed Ryan to begin by telling his mother all that he'd heard about the man's voice, and he did.

Dylan followed up, explaining who Roman Hadley was, his strange connection to them, and the fact that they were now learning from her son that Hadley was a listener also. Under normal circumstances, she would not be privy to such information regarding the society, but these were not normal circumstances, and her son might be in danger as a result of this person. Dylan also explained that they believed Ryan; they had proof of his abilities.

"Great," she said. "But you know what? This is my fault, anyway. Had I never brought him to you all in the first place, none of this would be happening. This is precisely why I didn't want my son connected or identified in any way. Do you see that now, Ryan?"

"Please, don't," Susan said. "Blaming him, or yourself, won't make his psychic abilities disappear. I understand your fear, your frustration. We can work through this, I promise. Please let me help you; this is what I do."

Annie sighed in what almost felt like relief, but more like abandon. It was not that she felt a momentary like for Susan Logan; it was because she had nowhere to turn, nowhere to hide from it anymore. Everything that had been hidden was suddenly coming into the light. She had no other choice; her son's safety was now in question.

"You know," Dylan said to her, "you might want to tell us exactly why you're so afraid of Ryan's ability."

"No, not right now," Susan interrupted. "Let's save that for later. Right now, why don't we discuss how to go about investigating Hadley? What should we do? Do we call the police or the FBI? I mean, Hadley was with the FBI once wasn't he?"

They mentioned alerting the rest of the board members in case they heard from Hadley, and the fact that all they had to go on, or give to the authorities, was Ryan's proficiency in remote hearing. While that might be good enough for the board, it wouldn't work for the police, although the FBI had been acquainted with remote hearing.

Annie wrapped her arm around her son's shoulders, while sadness streaked across her face. Ryan then broke the congested silence that followed the deep discussion.

"I have to go to the bathroom."

There was light laughter. Susan agreed, suggesting a quick break. They rose from the table to momentarily adjourn. Ryan walked out the door as they were cleaning up and walked down the hall—to the men's room.

* * * *

Like most public men's rooms, the light was on when he entered. The sterile smell of hospital clean invaded his nostrils as he stood at one of the urinals. Two stalls stood at his left, and though he could see no feet underneath, he fought a strange sensation of a presence in there. When he finished, he turned his head sideways to look again—no feet, no shadows.

He washed his hands at the sink as he always did, then pulled two brown paper towels, the kind that smelled like cardboard, from the dispenser and wiped his hands dry. There were no sounds around, at least there weren't over the running water and the thrashing paper. Then there were no sounds at all as the deafness occurred.

He hadn't expected it now. His body numbed, stunned into distraction, the paper towels falling to the floor. He lifted his head up, as though listening to a voice from above. It was his father...

"Ryan! Get out! Leave that room, right now!"

His breathing heaved up and down as the fear struck him instantly. He tried to run for the door, but strong hands grabbed him from behind. Suddenly, all he could smell now was the scent of almonds, thick and heavy through his nostrils, and instantly, he fell fast asleep in the arms of a stranger.

* * * *

Annie sat in the lounge with Brett and Dylan, nervously listening to their conversation about this Hadley person and stunned at what was unfolding. The more she heard, the more she thought of her son being stalked by someone with the same ability; it was unthinkable. For just a passing second, she wished Ian were here. She continued to sit and stare, mesmerized by the fears that gripped her heart and the thoughts that ravaged her mind.

Susan and the Leeds girl returned from the ladies' room that had only been a quick jaunt across the hall. It had been five minutes since Ryan ventured to the same general area.

"So, have we decided whether to call the FBI, at least to run a check on Hadley?"

Susan asked the team, as though a decision had already been reached. What seemed to trouble Annie even more was that the team had no doubts about Ryan. If they had, maybe this whole thing would go away.

"You know, this is all starting to make sense," Dylan said to the rest. "Hadley seemed to know everything, where we were, what we were doing; he knew things about Tracy Kimball, and details of our cases before we divulged anything. Of course he's a listener, and you know, Sidney suspected him of having some type of psychic ability."

"He's been listening, or should I say, 'eavesdropping,' on us the entire time," Leah said, angrily.

They began talking more about Hadley and to what secret project Ryan could possibly be referring.

Ryan. She was snapped out of her reverie by the thought of her son. She looked at her watch; ten minutes had passed since Ryan went to the restroom.

"Did either of you see Ryan in the hallway?" She asked the two ladies, who hadn't.

She pointed to her watch.

"He's been gone for ten minutes. What could be taking him so long?"

Her tone was not yet alarm, but concern. They exchanged glances, as though they knew she was right.

"I'll go and check on him," Brett said, casually, hinting at overreaction. He stood from the table and left the lounge in search of Ryan.

Susan resumed the conversation, telling her that she wanted to schedule a session with everyone present, including Ryan. Annie nodded her head in distracted consent, keeping her eyes focused on the door.

* * * *

Brett pushed the door of the men's room open and walked inside; it was silent except for the sound of the whooshing vacuum pull of the door as he entered.

"Ryan?" His voice bounced off the tiled walls and echoed back to him. "Ryan, are you in here?"

He walked past the sinks and the mirror, oblivious of the paper towels on the floor, and approached the urinals—no one.

"Ryan?" He called out again as he reached the stalls, knocking on the first of two. "Ryan, are you in there?" The stall door was ajar, and with a tap, he pushed it back. No one was inside. Quickly he pushed the second stall door open, and again, no one was there. Where was he?

His heart began to race at the thought that was now looming as a reality. How could he be lost, he was only right down the hallway? Brett strode fast for the exit, and then noticed two paper towels on the floor.

He swung the door wide behind him as he ran out, calling Ryan's name aloud through the hospital hallway. The same nurse who had kept them posted on Sidney's condition ran over to him.

"Mr. Taylor, what's wrong?"

"Did you see that kid that was with us in the lounge? He walked down here to the men's room, and he's been gone for ten minutes. He's not in there..."

"Well, maybe he's back in the lounge?"

Brett sighed in irritation of her. Why did all stupid questions come in times of emergency? No, he thought, there was no way he could have missed him.

He flung the lounge door open and looked inside—no Ryan. The looks of expectancy on their faces greeted him in anticipation. He hated being the bearer of bad news, confirming that instinct that Annie wore well on her face.

"Ryan's gone!"

Collective gasps showered the lounge like steam, and they jumped from their chairs at the words that Brett nearly shouted. Dylan ran past Brett and out into hallway, suspecting that some silly oversight was the issue, or maybe Ryan had gone down to the hospitality shop. Leah trailed behind him.

Susan grasped Brett by the shoulders with a firm hold.

"Tell us everything," she said.

Brett looked at Annie, who was standing from her chair, frozen, her frenzied, fearful eyes hoping for a mistake. He suddenly felt the guilt of assuring Ryan that he'd be safe with them in a hospital.

"I'm so sorry. I couldn't find him," he said to her.

"Brett," Susan cried, "Tell us!"

He told how he'd gone to the men's room, and how it had been vacant—Ryan was nowhere inside. The only thing he'd found were two paper towels on the floor, but anyone could have dropped them.

"Well, he could still be here," Susan said. "He may have wandered off somewhere."

"That's right," Dylan said. "Leah and I are going to look for him. He may have gone down to the hospitality shop, and it's very easy to get lost around here. Let's not overreact yet. I mean, Ryan did sneak off to come here, didn't he?"

Brett could see that the notion didn't console Annie at all. He went over to her and put his arm around her. The tears welled up in her eyes.

"Not this time," she said. "I had the oddest feeling before I sent you to look for him. I've got to go find him!"

Suddenly, she ran out of the lounge and into the hallway, screaming for her son.

* * * *

"Ryan! Ryan!"

Her screams rang out through the hospital floor as she burst from the lounge in unhinged panic. Heads turned toward her, and two nurses ran to her sides, catching her flailing body and holding her. Susan realized that the situation had now gone beyond rationalization. If Ryan was kidnapped from this hospital, it was her job to act immediately; she had no other choice.

Two armed, hospital security guards ran to the scene, approaching Susan.

"Security, get the hospital in lock-down, immediately! We have a child missing, and there is reason to believe he was kidnapped from this hospital, in between now and fifteen minutes ago. I will notify our chief, Dr. Kemp."

The officers nodded and radioed down to the security hub. Suddenly, all electric doors in the hospital automatically closed by computerized command, the matching glass gateways interlocking with a loud beeping that meant safe, secure, but also quarantine. The officers continued to radio, and a hospital security search ensued.

Susan ordered a nurse to sedate Annie, whose screams grew louder in protest, but still the syringe found its way into her arm.

"Annie, we're all going to find him," Susan reassured her. "But right now, you are in no condition to." She had her admitted into a room, and soon a wheelchair whisked Annie away, the sedative quickly setting by the sign of sinking eyelids.

Dylan and Leah stepped off the elevator, arriving back from the hospitality shop, the lobby, the vending machines, and any other area to which Ryan could have wandered.

"We couldn't find him," Dylan said. "He's gone."

"I know. The hospital is now in lock-down," she said.

"Susan?" Behind her, Greg Talbot approached. The nurse had said he'd be by soon. "What's going on? What's this about a lockdown?"

"Long story, but there was a guest here for Sidney, a child. We suspect he was kidnapped from the hospital only moments ago."

"I take it this has something to do with my patient?" Greg asked in a stern, authoritative manner.

"Yes, it does," she said.

"Then Sidney is not to hear one word of this, at least, not now anyway."

"Sidney?" She asked, almost forgetting amid the confusion. "You mean?"

"That's what I came to tell you all. Sidney Pratt is awake."

Chapter Eight

Quick embraces of relief were exchanged at the news: Sidney was going to be all right. Brett looked upward, thanking God, and Leah hung her head as the tears dropped from her eyes.

"When can we see him?" Susan asked, dropping her hands from the lower part of her face where she'd held them in joyful surprise.

"I will let two of you in at a time," he said. "But when you go in there, remember that he is still in recovery; there is to be no excitement, no pressure, and not a word of what has happened here, understand?"

They agreed, and Talbot left, promising to return when he felt his patient was ready to see them. Then, hospital security approached Susan.

"Dr. Logan, we've conducted a search of the hospital grounds, inside and out; we've turned up nothing. We're about to notify the police."

"On second thought," she said. "I insist that the FBI be called instead. The Bureau will have better knowledge of this situation given the circumstances of it, and because there is a suspect in this case, they may use more discretion, which may be important in finding the boy. I will be treating the boy's mother, so I am her attending physician."

"Right away, Dr. Logan." The main security officer stepped away, radioing her instructions as ordered. The same attending nurse approached her just then.

"Dr. Talbot says two of you may go in first to see Sidney, Dr. Logan, but not more than five minutes."

Susan thanked her, and then decided that she and Dylan should go first; Leah and Brett returned to the lounge. As the nurse led them through two extended corridors to the ICU, Susan and Dylan remained quiet, hopeful, and careful to suppress any hint of fraught emotions in front of him.

The ICU was a collection of triage units assembled in close proximity next to each other in a classic hospital ward setting. Random beeping co-existed with the sounds of pulsing respirators and the soft-spoken tones of patients and nurses. There was a fear here, just as present as the sickly smell, and Susan could sense it. The look on Dylan's face silently agreed.

Sidney's eyes were closed in soft slumber, his body tucked tightly into the bed that seemed to be a part of him. He looked defenseless without his glasses, his face puffed and swollen, and layers of white bandage wrapped securely around the crown of his head. Susan recognized the fear on Dylan's face at seeing him, so she leaned over to Sidney's ear and softly whispered his name.

His eyelids fluttered open and gazed back at her.

"Sidney? How is my little boy?" That's exactly what she felt he was at this moment. No matter how much older he'd become through the years, she kept seeing the little boy that came into her office around twenty years ago with two prodigal parents both afraid and resentful of him.

"Susan." His voice was soft, sleepy, and dry.

"That's right," she said. "And Dylan is here too."

"Hey, Sid," he whispered, stepping forward, trying to control the creaking in his voice. "You gave us all one hell of a scare. You've got to relax and get better for us."

Sidney seemed to answer with a motioning movement of his eyes. Then, the first question he asked caught them both off guard.

"Where's Ryan?" His words were slow and slurred, but unmistakable. Susan sat speechless and turned her head toward Dylan. His wide-eyed alarm relayed to her that he was as equally dumbfounded and scrambling for the right response. She turned back to Sidney.

"Ryan is okay, Sidney. He wants to see you as soon as it's possible, but you have to rest now. Brett and Leah may be in to see you also. You know we've all been here for you." The question she was sure he would ask came next.

"What happened?"

"You had a cerebral hemorrhage, Sidney. You've had surgery, and according to the doctor, you're going to be fine." She detected a slight scoff under his weakened breath that told her Sidney Pratt would pull through. She instructed him to get more rest, and told him they would return soon.

"Don't worry about anything, Sid," Dylan said. "Everything's under control."

They left the ICU as he closed his eyes again, and once they were a significant length down the hall, they turned to face each other.

"I'm not very comfortable with the fact that you just lied to him," Dylan said. "Sidney knows something is amiss—that's just him; it's the way he is. And you didn't even know Ryan before tonight; you don't think he picked up on that?"

"What do you suggest I should have done, tell him the truth? 'Well, gee, Sidney, I'm sorry, but Ryan was abducted from this hospital. But everything's okay, we'll find him.' Really, Dylan, do you want him to have a setback, another hemorrhage? 'Everything is under control.' Why didn't you just tell him everything for chrissake?"

"According to Ryan, Sidney heard him the night of the accident. What if Ryan is calling out to Sidney now? If so, there's a chance we could find him."

Susan stopped walking at the realization, and then turned to him, issuing a frustrated sigh.

"Dylan, we are just going to have to wait and see."

* * * *

It was Brett and Leah's turn to see Sidney, and the same sight greeted them upon entering the room. Leah's breath quivered at the ache in her chest at seeing him. She stared at him and wondered what she would have done without him. His sleepy eyes seemed unsurprised when they opened, and his visitors laughed and sighed in relief at the tiny smile that cracked across his face.

"It's true, you know," he said, eyeing them as they stood on either side of him.

"What's true, Sid?" Leah asked, looking at Brett.

"What they say about your life flashing before your eyes when you die."

"Yeah, but you're not dead, Sid." Brett said, cautiously teasing him.

"Came pretty damn close," he said.

Leah's face hardened at his accuracy. He was right, and she knew it. Images of him lying on the floor, silent and moribund in the blood that soaked the floor beneath him flashed through her mind. How she wished she could clear her mind completely.

Sidney obviously saw the mounting stress and turmoil on her face because he asked her what was wrong. She looked up, unable to lie to him, as they were kindred spirits, connected through their fates. Susan had advised her and Brett not to say a word about Ryan's disappearance. Any shock or stress could cause Sidney to relapse, but she would do her best to be discreet.

"I have been worried about you, what else?" She thought for a moment to tell him about the visions that had been plaguing her, then thought better of it. His eyes cast a suspicious sideways glance at her, so she spoke fast, changing the subject before it began.

"What is the last thing you remember, Sidney?"

"I was getting ready to meet you," he said in a euphoric lull. "The pain in my head...was worse. There was static...I heard Tracy...pipeline." He swallowed to moisten his parched mouth. "Then there was blood." He kept his eyes closed for a few seconds, as though erasing unwanted memories.

"Tracy Kimball made a pipeline connection after she died?" Brett was surprised to hear this, but kept his voice at a soft, tranquil minimum. Sidney responded with an affirmative hum through his closed lips.

"I saw her on the other side when I almost died," he said. "I saw her, David, my grandfather...I saw us."

"You saw us?" Leah asked, but her heart sank as she silently realized that Sidney's life really had flashed before him. *That's how close we came to losing him,* she thought. "Well, you're going to be out of here, soon, Sid. So, get some rest. We can't stay long."

He nodded his head, and she kissed him on the cheek. She and Brett had made it out of the room with no mention of Ryan.

* * * *

His head didn't hurt, not the way it had before. He felt wasted, immovable, and his visitors, as well as the nurses that checked on him, confirmed that he was, in fact, alive. He had made it back; his grandfather had told him he would. There were no more corridors, no more strange light, just the inside of University Hospital that he knew well.

After Leah and Brett had left, he fought to open his eyes and think quickly before he dozed off again. They were hiding something—all of them. He could tell by Susan's slow responses and Dylan's lack of them, the look of terror and turmoil on Leah's face, and the strange way Brett kept looking away. Something was up, but what?

Tracy had told him that he had to save Ryan. He knew what he had seen was real; Tracy had never known, nor heard of Ryan Quinn, yet she was insistent that he must help him.

Danger. She had used that word.

As he wondered more about Ryan, the sleep began to take over once again, and the thought was no more.

* * * *

After seeing Sidney, the four of them reconvened back in the lounge, exasperated from the day's chaotic events and unaware that outside, dusk had turned to nightfall. Only moments had passed before a tall, blond man entered the lounge and approached them. He was told exactly where to find them—and he had. The man with the unfamiliar face walked right to the long table where they sat; he nodded his head in greeting.

"Dr. Susan Logan?" He addressed her, his leather wallet readied in his hand.

"Yes, I'm Dr. Logan," she said, rising from the table.

"Agent Wiley; FBI," he said, flipping open his wallet and displaying his ID. "We were notified that a child went missing from this hospital tonight."

Agent Stuart Wiley was one of the Bureau's top veteran's, experienced in missing person's cases, and somewhat intimidating at six foot-three and a rough, stony, expressionless face of fifty-five years.

"Yes," she said. "Ryan Quinn is his name. His mother had to be admitted when she realized he went missing. You see, Agent Wiley, Ryan is what's known as a clairaudient, and at one time, was being studied by the university's Paranormal Research and Investigative society."

She motioned to the three sitting alongside her at the table, and Agent Wiley drew an empty chair and sat with them. She explained who Sidney was and Ryan's connection to him, as well as how Ryan had come to be at the hospital. She knew the FBI was experienced with remote psychic studies, and that's why she felt they were the obvious choice to deal with the situation.

"Well," Agent Wiley said. "I know that the Bureau disbanded all of its research projects on the subject back in the seventies."

"We can also identify a suspect in this case," Susan said. "In fact, we think he may have been FBI at one time. His name is Roman Hadley."

Wiley's eyes stared directly at her; his eyebrows arched upward in some unspoken recognition. Dylan described Ryan's insistence when the boy was brought to the lounge, and how Hadley was one of the heads leading the society, yet no one had ever seen him. Then, Wiley stunned them with what he said next.

"You should know that Roman Hadley was never an FBI agent; that is part of his false identity. We have been investigating and searching for this 'Roman Hadley' for years. Whoever this man really is, he has been using, and hiding behind your society, and you seem to have found him for us."

Shock was once again unleashed, as this day and night became one and the same of endless confusion. The FBI had been investigating Roman Hadley all along, and they sat reeling from the realization that they'd been in the dark, unaware. Wiley's words were spoken with an uncompromising and straightforward directness. He spared no time or feelings.

"This person calling himself Hadley was part of a rogue group of psychics that broke away from the Bureau's remote psychic experiments in the late sixties, early seventies. They were a small group that wanted to expand the studies further than the FBI was willing to coordinate, or explore, so they successfully disappeared from the view of the government. Apparently, they continued studying and researching in some underground fashion, whether figurative or literal, and working toward an agenda involving the retrieval of top-secret government information, security plans, trade secrets, mainly through the use of the highest order of remote listeners and viewers. All of it, a grand scheme of psychic espionage conducted under our nation's radar for decades.

"Their ultimate goal is to create a state of national and world security that would rival everything we have so far, triumphing in their psychic research and pursuits. Though what goal they would hope to ascertain beyond that point is anyone's guess: world domination, mass financial embezzlement, toppling governments, who knows?

"All information that was recorded about the participants of that time has either led to dead ends, been lost, or wasn't much in the first place. We don't think Hadley was one of the original members, but he came aboard at some time in the late sixties. The fact that he posed as an FBI agent actually worked in his favor for a while; it was like being right under our noses, as they say. But, it didn't work forever. The agency eventually discovered more than a few imposters within our framework, one leading to another, then others.

"Roman Hadley, as I'm sure you were all aware, is said to be an extremely capable remote listener that has managed to evade us for over thirty years."

"We didn't know that Hadley was a listener until today," Dylan interrupted, explaining that when Ryan revealed what he'd heard, it was only then that they had put it together, and then it had all made sense.

"Sidney had suspected that Hadley possessed some sort of psychic ability," he explained further. "He said that Hadley seemed to know everything as it happened."

"He knew details of our cases," Leah chimed in, "as we were working on them, and we hadn't told him the particulars yet."

"He seemed to know our every move also," Brett said. "That is what triggered Sidney's suspicion. He even thought Hadley might have been 'listening.'"

"So none of you ever found it suspicious that you never actually laid eyes on Roman Hadley?"

"Sort of," Dylan said. "But he always kept in touch, and—"

"We thought he was a former agent," Leah said, as though Wiley had forgotten. "And overall, when we spoke to him, he sounded like a very nice man. Sidney is the one who initiated the suspicion, what there was of it."

"What about his interest in your society? Didn't you all wonder what that might have been?" His tone was not accusatory, but persistent to understand.

"Again, Agent Wiley," Dylan said. "He did mention once working in the area of remote listening with the FBI; we assumed it was as an agent, not as a participant. You see our board members have various reasons why they maintain an interest in our society through their patronage. Some have had their own experiences; some are buffs who love excitement. We also have an author on our board whose interest is research. Hadley's reason fit right in."

"Dr. Logan, I understand you haven't been on the board that long?"

"I was inducted only a few days ago."

"So, as a board member, you haven't met Hadley, either?"

"No, I haven't."

"All right, then what we're going to do first," Wiley said, "is place tracers on all of your phone lines at the university, as well as your personal phones in case Hadley tries to contact any of you."

"Look, that's fine," Leah said, "anything to find Ryan. But what you must understand, Agent Wiley, is that if Roman Hadley is a listener, which we are now convinced that he is, you can bet that he is listening right now to this very conversation."

Wiley's face seemed to soften, as though he hadn't considered that one.

"That's right," Dylan said. "We can now prove that he has been listening with his remote ear to us the entire time we've known him."

"That may be so," Wiley conceded. "But there may be the slightest chance that he will call in; if so, we need to be prepared."

"You all don't think Hadley would hurt Ryan, do you?" Susan's question was directed at the team, who stayed silent.

"His goal is not to hurt him," Wiley said. "His goal is to use him, to hone him, to make him the perfect listener. He is aware of the boy's talents, and he will try to exploit them to the fullest. Ryan is much too valuable to him to harm a single hair on his head."

"Let's hope so," Susan said. "Because I'm not so sure what will become of his mother. I think there is a lot of guilt there. She may be blaming herself for this."

"Either way," Wiley said, "when can I speak to Sidney Pratt or the mother?"

The words increased the tension in the room. The cards they were trying to hide were now being forced from their hands, though they couldn't sidestep Sidney forever.

"Dr. Talbot says that Sidney is not to hear a word of Ryan's disappearance yet," Susan said. "He fears a setback, if he does. You will just have to discuss an appropriate time with him. As far as Annie Quinn is concerned, I can tell you that I have not yet had the chance to examine her. She's been sedated and won't wake until tomorrow. I will let you know."

Wiley nodded in understanding. Brett told Wiley everything that had occurred from the moment Ryan left the lounge, to the point where he himself entered the men's room, finding nothing but paper towels on the floor. They then walked together, retracing Brett's steps.

When they returned to the lounge, Wiley described how the search for Ryan was now in place, and how both Sidney and Annie were now under surveillance for their own protection. He asked to accompany the team back to the university, having requested from them a copy of Ryan's file and all information concerning Hadley. They complied, and together they left the hospital.

Susan made her way back to the office, secretly thankful that this disastrous day was drawing to a close.

* * * *

She sat in her office, unwinding for a few quiet moments before she left the hospital, thinking about Sidney lying there helpless. Susan thought back and remembered why her interest in him had been roused all those years ago; it was when she realized what he was. She'd never told Sidney, but Mark, her fiancé, the same man that Sidney heard that day in her office, had possessed the same ability—clairaudience.

When they were teenagers, she had witnessed Mark's psychic ability. He had heard the voices of the dead and even the living. He was able to hear everything from loved ones who passed, to the occasional comment made by a classmate distances away. She recalled how the whole thing had frightened his family and himself to some extent. He even swore himself against it, which had been fine with her. She loved him for who he was.

She had never seen him again after he'd left for Vietnam; he was reported MIA, and when the young Sidney mentioned him the way he had, she knew he had made contact. The shock of that moment had turned her world upside down. So, privately, she devoted herself to the study of such psychic abilities and paranormal phenomena. She had to learn more, and soon, it had encompassed her life, enveloping her every moment; for if life did continue afterward, the prospect of proving it would be immense.

Through the years, especially after the last American POW was released from captivity, she assumed that Mark's status was changed to KIA. It wouldn't surprise her; Sidney had heard him the same way that Mark had heard others all those years ago. Obviously, Mark was dead, but Sidney had brought back so much of him that it made her content, relieved to know that in some way, Mark waited for her.

Now she sat at her desk reading the society's file on Ryan that

Dylan had emailed her. In so many ways, Ryan reminded her of Sidney, and Sidney of Mark, as though they were all connected. She realized how Ryan was more in touch with his telepathic side, being able to hear the living also, much like Mark. This fact made them both different types of clairaudients from Sidney; Sidney only heard the dead.

But something struck her; Ryan told Dylan that Sidney heard him when he projected with his mind the night of Tracy's accident. How could Ryan be sure? She would have to ask Sidney himself when the time came...soon.

She noticed a notation in Ryan's file...

Subject's mother has terminated all sessions with the society.

Just like Sidney's parents, she thought, *fear.* She would have to address Annie's fear as soon as she was able to, but for now, Annie was safe here in the hospital. The FBI was working fast to pinpoint Roman Hadley's whereabouts, and there was nothing more she could do tonight. She would catch up on Ryan's file at home, where she was headed to call it a day, once and for all.

Chapter Nine

He awoke, groggy and half-slumbering, lazing in the comfort of the soft bed within the dimly lit nest that had been prepared for him. He lay lulled by the pallid glow and the warmth of the room that coaxed him into the comfortable acceptance of his surroundings. He swallowed, heaved, and coughed as the taste and smell of almonds still lingered like the stink of the skunk that sprayed him once in the woods.

Ryan tried to pull his thoughts together into one cohesive binding, but all recollections seemed to be lost, evading him like the flying creatures he strived to catch in the video game. He was so sure he'd gone to the hospital to see Sidney, but he must have fallen asleep. Yet, he was there, because Mom had followed him; she must have brought him home. He went to the men's room, and then...what had happened next?

Someone grabbed him from behind...

Ryan threw himself up from the single bed that was not his own. Terror swept him with the invisible pricks of pins and needles down the length of his body, and panic pushed his breath out in rushing gasps. This was not his room. The overhanging lamp that clouded the light it housed, causing the comfortable dimness, was not his. The dim light displayed a room devoid of anything except the bed, the light, and a small table and matching chair.

Where am I? It was the only thought he could muster as all others were obliterated by the barrage of paranoia, panic, and fear. His eyes fought to focus, but the blurriness made everything fuzzy, and the fuzziness fought his focusing eyes. He could make out the door to the room with its small, rectangular window through which he saw nothing but outside light. He couldn't look anymore; the strain caused a pain in his eyelids.

So, the man had found him. Had he been hiding in the hospital, waiting for him?

"Help!" His scream echoed through the small room, and he was answered with only the minor refrain of his own voice returning. He called out again, but no opposite sound responded.

He fell back on the bed as the dizziness turned his stomach. He dry-heaved again and swallowed hard, the sweat spanning in rivulets across his forehead. He let his breathing simmer with exhales through his mouth that quelled the queasiness. Now he would focus with his mind. If the man couldn't hear his screams, he could hear him another way.

And Sidney, he would also call out to Sidney.

The snugness of the bed combined with the dimness of the overhanging lamp and the soft purr of the heating system cajoled him into relaxing, resting, and remembering to focus. He remained still, lulling his body into peace and initiating his mind into action.

Sidney...

The soft silent thought projected out into a vast, unhearing world.

* * * *

Roman Hadley sat nervously behind his long mahogany desk, his left hand resting comfortably against his chin, wrinkles of wonder etched into his expression. He'd just received word that the mission had been accomplished. The boy, Ryan, was safe in the prepared haven where he would remain hidden. Amid the relief that his plan was moving into action, lingered an overt skepticism, a profound ruefulness that crept through his heart at the situation.

He would never harm Ryan, nor was that the intention. A part of him did not want to see the boy imprisoned into the same underground and clandestine existence that his life had been. He tried to override those thoughts, but felt himself becoming angrier at the repetitive realization that he'd spent years waiting for a way out.

It took an immense amount of concentration to suppress the thought that when the time was absolute, he would abandon Ryan with the secret society then disappear. It was the only option, as the group would never agree to an exchange. Then, he would contact her, and together they could bring down this endless and sinister assemblage.

It had to be done; he refused to spend the rest of his life cloaking his thoughts from the others. If they knew what he was thinking now, they would kill him. He could bring them down when he was once again on the outside. She would help him.

After all, she wasn't far away...

He swerved his leather chair around to face the cabinet on the wall behind him, and with the touch of a button, the cabinet doors parted, revealing three security monitors in the form of small television sets. The black and white image on the first of the screens displayed an uneventful live depiction facing the outside of the underground compound; the second showed the door to the room where he was kept, and the third was a much closer view of Ryan, asleep but stirring on the bed.

He was awakening, slowly gaining his faculties as the effects of the chloroform were subsiding, Hadley thought. He guessed that the boy had already discovered his strange and unfamiliar whereabouts, but remained unable to respond physically. He would soon be fully cognizant, and when he was, Hadley would distract him as best as possible.

There would be many things Ryan would need to hear, to learn, and eventually come to appreciate. It would be a difficult undertaking, especially with someone so young, someone so close to his mother, his only family, but Hadley would try to appeal to the boy's fascination with his ability, his eagerness to learn. Then through continuous adulation, he would instill in Ryan a self-esteem that hopefully, would spark an obsession, creating a strong desire and willingness to proceed.

Unfortunately, Hadley was now the one distracted after listening for the boy's location this evening. It was *her* voice that he'd unexpectedly heard with the others...and with the boy. Her connection to Ryan had been an unexpected development, and he wondered if his proximity right now was too close, close enough that her involvement with Ryan might endanger her from those who were listening. Now, he wished deep inside that he'd searched for a way out many years ago, even if it meant being killed or disposed of—like an ineffective, damaged product. He would make it easy to find Ryan when the time came.

And so Sidney Pratt was awake. He felt relief that his continuously intrusive searches of Sidney's mind had not killed him, but it would be only a matter of time before the boy called out to him. Then they would be looking for Ryan, and him, as they were now aware of his involvement, and that he was also a listener, the mastermind orchestrating the secret society and indulging in new-age psychic espionage.

After all the years of working with the highly sophisticated team of investigators, it was time to lose them, to abandon all contact. Their next case was to find him, and they were the best in their field. Once he vanished, he would see to it that Ryan was located and saved. He hoped it would be possible, and equally possible that he would survive this mutiny; yet a quiet dread within his heart seemed to whisper otherwise.

* * * *

Wiley's habit of gulping steaming hot coffee came in handy after being up all night studying the file on Ryan Quinn that Dylan had faxed him, as well as the files of cases that Hadley had directed and was subsequently briefed on. There hadn't been much to gain from the latter files, but Wiley had been amazed at the extent of Ryan Quinn's ability, as documented by the team. It was a unique psychic endowment, a direct parallel to Hadley's own. There was no doubt that Ryan was seen as a valuable asset to this hidden society.

Not having joined the Bureau until 1980, Wiley hadn't been part of the FBI's investigations into remote viewing and hearing, nor did he ever maintain any interest in paranormal occurrences or abilities. But in 1987, he was one of the agents assigned to the highly secretive and controversial case of a psychic rogue group that had broken away from the FBI's remote psychic projects; they had branched out on their own, achieving success by obtaining classified information and other forms of espionage.

Through the years, he researched remote viewing, clairaudience, clairvoyance, and many other psychic abilities and paranormal occurrences. He never gave the issues much thought or belief until meeting some of the subjects the Bureau had studied at the time, who fully demonstrated their abilities for him. He had also worked with psychics on missing persons' cases, some of whom were acclaimed and proven successes.

Then one day the Bureau came up with a name, an imposter masquerading as one of them, passing right under their radar—Roman Hadley. Wiley was among a gathering of agents that had searched for years, unable to locate the elusive mastermind. He had no idea when he went to the hospital last night that the missing child had anything to do with the university's paranormal investigative society. When Susan Logan mentioned the name of the man he'd searched years for, he felt the twitching of his soul, as if some force reached inside and tried to snatch it from him. He was stunned into silence. Hadley was right in front of them the whole time.

Now Wiley wondered if Hadley was looking for a way out after all these years, planning to induct the boy as his ultimate replacement—a possible theory. If so, it might be easy to corner him before he disappeared altogether. That would be much easier if he were to discover Hadley's original and true identity, a task the Bureau had tried to accomplish for years and failed.

It seemed as though the man was nobody at all before he became Roman Hadley. What little information was gathered from the discovery of an underground compound in Washington, DC, had identified persons only as "subjects," and therefore led to nothing. They could only guess that Hadley had been there.

The waitress in Ed's Diner came and refilled his coffee, interrupting his thoughts for a moment. He always came here and sat alone at a table, pondering details and sequences of events. A meeting was scheduled with the investigative team, and Susan Logan, today at the university at 1:00 pm. He glanced at his watch—12:30. He would interview them further about the events the night before, as he was still unable to speak with either Sidney Pratt or Annie Quinn.

The agents investigating the scene last night had turned up a sliver of information, and he was about to share that with the team; although, it wasn't much to go on. There could always be something, some minute detail they might remember about Hadley that may work in finding him. Sometimes, people didn't understand how significant something small really was. He would find out soon. He finished his second cup of coffee, paid the check, and left for the university.

* * * *

The voice was soft and faint, a whisper, but it woke him. He rolled his eyes around the room—no one was there. The night before, after everyone left, he thought he'd heard someone say his name, but it was hard to tell. Between the weakness and the pain medication, Sidney slumbered in and out, unable to stay awake for long.

He felt better today than when he was last awake, and he felt sure that the soft voice called his name...*Sidney...*

The more he thought on it, the more it sounded like Ryan, yet Ryan wasn't here. Funny, Dylan didn't seem surprised when he asked about Ryan. Susan had answered for him, and she didn't even know Ryan Quinn. Then again, being a psychiatrist, she could have been controlling the situation, seeing to it that he didn't stress himself.

Something was going on—but what?

He would concern himself with it later. Right now, his eyes were closing again, slipping him back into his restful abode.

* * * *

The team sat inside their headquarters, along with Susan, waiting for Agent Wiley, who had called a meeting with the four of them. Their faces were only slightly rested after the long day and night that preceded today. Glum faces glanced over at the door when a steady knock came at exactly one o'clock; Wiley arrived on time—down to the minute.

Once inside, Dylan extended him the courtesy of his own regular seat at the head of the long conference table, since Wiley would be addressing them. After helping themselves to coffee, (and yet another for Wiley) they reported to him that Hadley's number was disconnected, and the solitary email address they had for him had returned emails as unknown.

"Yes, I figured as much," he said, then continued. "Our agents questioned most of everyone working at the hospital last night; no one saw anything inside. The person who took Ryan, be it Hadley, or a hired hand, did an extremely inconspicuous job of it—undoubtedly professional. We spoke with potential witnesses outside the hospital, and we may have a lead from a woman who was there in the parking lot last night, picking up a friend.

"At approximately 8:15, she saw someone carrying, with both hands, one of those large, hefty hospital laundry sacks out of the building. This person then carefully placed the sack into the backseat of a waiting limousine, and then got inside via the same door. The car drove off immediately. She said she first took notice because of the fancy stretch; she admired it for a few seconds then turned away, and when she looked back, she saw the person out of nowhere. She found it strange the way he carried the sack and even stranger the way he so cautiously handled it, placing it into, of all things, a limo.

"I'm almost positive that Ryan was inside that laundry sack." Again, Wiley was abrupt and to the point, the sound of his revelation bringing sighs of tension, tears of fear, and hung heads in trepidation.

"The witness was positive it was a male, but couldn't see his face too well in the dark or from the position in which she was parked. Given this information, we can be sure that Hadley is behind the kidnapping, and he isn't stupid enough, or young enough, to carry this out on his own. He has accomplices: the man carrying the sack, the driver—question is, how many?

"Let's also keep in mind that Hadley is not out to hurt Ryan; he can't afford to. Ryan is an extremely valuable asset to this rogue group; they need his ability. Finding Ryan, to them, is like winning the mega-lottery. He is also young, and with his ability at a peaking point, they can study him extensively with less resistance than an adult.

"Obviously, Hadley discovered Ryan through working with your society. I believe that Hadley then reported Ryan's information to the group, and he may want to use Ryan as a trade-off for his own services—just a theory, anyway."

"So, you don't think Hadley is the leader of this group?" Dylan asked, confused.

"Well, he is the one in charge, let's say. That doesn't mean he is the ultimate overseer. I think he reports back to an authority, whether there is one or more, I can't say. But for Hadley to receive a false identity as an agent, then live successfully without being detected..." He paused. "Let's just say that someone higher up has provided it."

"You mean someone in the *government*?" Susan asked with incredulous disbelief.

"Well, doctor," Wiley hissed at her assumption. "That would be difficult to say or even pinpoint for that matter. I mean, whoever began fueling this rogue group may have been FBI, or of some higher authority. We couldn't know that at this point. Many of the people even distantly connected with the Bureau's psychic projects, at that time, have been investigated. Many of them are dead, and some have continued to lead normal, explainable, innocent lives; any remaining leads proved to be dead ends.

"Roman Hadley is the key to all of this. I think that if we bring down the main one, we bring them all down, like dominoes. Actually, I don't mean this the way it sounds, but Ryan's abduction may be just the situation the FBI needs to break this case once and for all."

"You mentioned that Hadley might be using Ryan as a trade-off for himself," Brett said. "Does that mean that you think Hadley himself may have been an unwilling participant all of these years?"

Wiley was impressed by the young man's perception.

"It's possible, yes. Though at some point, Hadley did come over to their side. We have proof of his handsome compensation that obviously eliminated the need for continuous coercion."

"How exactly would this group coax Ryan into submitting to them?" Leah asked, the others seeming to echo the concern.

"That is what scares me," Wiley said. "They would probably threaten his mother; she is his only family. They may threaten Sidney Pratt, which is why I need to see him as soon as possible. I need to find out if Ryan is still speaking to Sidney through clairaudient projection. We need to do everything we can to find this boy. I also noticed in Ryan's file that he is telepathic?"

"We seem to think so," Dylan said, then explained how Ryan was more in touch with his telepathic side than Sidney was, and that clairaudience was a form of telepathy. This, Wiley already knew.

"It's become apparent to me, as well as the rest of the Bureau, that this is going to be a very unusual case, one that is dependent upon the utilization of psychic abilities to help solve. In order to apprehend and dismantle this group, we are going to have to play their own game, by their own rules. They have gotten away with illegal conduct and dangerous exploits all of these years through the use of psychic ability; we are going to have to bring them down exactly the same way."

"We are all going to help in any way we can," Leah said.

"Great, because we are going to need it," Wiley said, and turned to Susan. "When can you get the Doc to let me see Sidney Pratt?"

"I don't know," she said. "It's only been a day—"

"Lean on him," he said. "Time is crucial. They may move Ryan to anywhere in the world, and if they do, we may never find him. What about the mother? If she wants to find her son, she needs to talk to me."

In the face of Wiley's frankness, Susan faltered. She knew he was right; after all, she couldn't let Annie withdraw. She needed to play an active role in finding her son.

"Let me check on her," she said. "I will set it up."

"Let's do it," Wiley said, and rose from his chair.

Chapter Ten

Annie sat up in her hospital bed, unable to feel the onslaught of the attacking nerves that surged inside her. She lingered, numb from the sedation, though it was not as heavy today. She had to find Ryan, but every time she managed to get out of bed, it was like floating, until her head grew heavy and her stomach turned. Then, she would allow herself to be tucked back into bed by the nurses, never having made it farther than the bathroom before whimpering with defeat.

Today, Susan Logan returned, telling her that an FBI agent named Wiley was here to see her, and that the search for Ryan was ongoing. Susan felt it best to have a meeting with the agent, here in her room, along with the investigators also. There was a coordinated and conscious effort to find Ryan, and the sooner they all met, the better. Annie agreed, and now all were assembled in chairs surrounding the bed in her hospital room.

The tall, blond man introduced himself as Agent Wiley of the FBI, the man heading the search and investigation into Ryan's abduction.

"We do have a potential suspect," Wiley said. He explained to her who Roman Hadley was, his role with the investigative society, and how he discovered Ryan. She knew most of the facts already, but still, the fact that the man was part of some secret psychic society who wanted to use her son for his ability blew her mind into magnified amazement. He explained to her how the group broke away from the FBI's remote psychic studies, surviving for years, studying subjects on their own, often against their will. Now they had laid their claim to her son.

"But, I want you to remain calm, Annie," he said. "Until now, we never had a strong enough link to locate them. This time we are going to find them because now they've made a catastrophic move on their behalf; they've kidnapped a child. We are going to nail Roman Hadley, and this group, and bring your son home. I promise."

A waterfall of tears washed down Annie's face in a lament of helpless abandon. Susan moved closer to her and held her hand, reassuring her. Then, Wiley spoke again.

"Annie," he said, in a surprisingly soft tone unmatched by his rugged countenance. "I would also like to explain that the FBI is on this exclusively from top to bottom. One of the reasons for that is, unlike a regular abduction, we cannot get the media involved in this, at least not yet. We remain unsure how large this group is, or how dangerous they can be. These people are powerfully proven psychic beings, possessing heightened states of abilities such as clairaudience, clairvoyance, and remote viewing.

"They're also criminal minds, conducting the highest order of national and possibly international espionage. One wrong move in our strategy, and they could relocate Ryan to anywhere in the world, and we may never find him. Hadley probably already knows that we're on to him, as he has virtually abandoned the investigative society, leaving no further contact. We have no idea how, or to what extent, Hadley and the group may be observing us right at this very moment.

She remembered a similar fear about Ian the day in the Library. The look on Annie's face betrayed her thoughts...

Then how the hell do you expect to find him?

"Annie, I know there are certain things you don't believe or subscribe to," Susan said, clutching her hand, "but, we are going to have to fight fire with fire. The team and I are going to work with the FBI as much as possible to find Ryan, and we will find him."

"So, my son's life depends on psychic abilities?" Her tone was one of expectancy, having known that sometime, someway, a moment like this would occur, and she would have to face the situation; though she'd never dreamed it would be of this magnitude. Secretly, she wished Ian were here right now; Ian would find his son.

"Annie, why don't we try to understand something?" Susan said, probing. "Tell us why you stopped the sessions between Ryan and the team a few years ago. Why didn't you want to understand your son's ability? Where did the fear come from, Annie?"

Here it was, the moment when everything would come into the light. The memories of Ian flashed through her mind: his being the happy man that she married, then later the drinking, the drugs, the fights, the screaming...his reading her mind. She remembered sneaking off to places because he'd kept her a mental prisoner. She recalled going to the library, searching the internet and skimming through all of the selected texts until she discovered what he was...a telepath.

She sighed with pain and glanced up at the ceiling. She was about to let it all go. She closed her eyes and breathed deeply before she began.

"When I first met Ian, Ryan's father, we were both young and in love," she said. "He was a good man then: warm, friendly, humorous, everything I had wanted. We had a few good years after we were married. Then, Ian changed. I noticed a difference in him: his looks, his attitude, his behavior.

"His drinking, which was never more than a few beers after work, became heavier; he would reek of alcohol when he finally did come home. While his drinking escalated, I discovered he was using cocaine, and soon enough, I watched the man I married disappear. Drugs and alcohol had completely changed him, and I had no idea why it all began. I searched my mind, thinking it was me or something I did, something I said, but it wasn't.

"I knew it wasn't about having a child because Ian was a great father. He loved Ryan; Ryan was his life. To this day, Ryan doesn't know about his father's demons. He was too young to notice or understand, and at the time, Ryan was the only thing that could bring his father back, if only for a few moments. I will never tell him about that part of his father, because it wasn't who his father really was.

"We began fighting. He became physically abusive, though I must admit, I was a fighter also. And then one night, something strange happened. We were fighting, and I said something about him inside my head. He heard every word I said. That was the first time, which I thought was only a coincidence.

"Eventually, I couldn't think around him; he read my thoughts, verbatim. He not only knew my whereabouts, but knew where I was planning on going, staying one step ahead of me, constantly, becoming the warden of the prison he'd made out of my life. Ryan was my only bargaining chip, and my own temper was my only defense.

"Then one day, I went to the library and read books about those types of people. I learned that Ian was a telepath, and from what I read, a very powerful one. I never noticed this ability in him when I first married him. I have always wondered whether it was always there, or whether something triggered it. To me, he had turned into the devil right before my eyes, and I had no idea why.

"I plotted a way out, and he knew, but he almost seemed too far gone to even hurt me anymore. He'd been out drinking one night, as usual, and I'd planned on taking Ryan and leaving in the morning, after Ian left for work. But after that night had unfolded, there was no longer any need."

She described Ryan waking up in the middle of the night, hysterical from the nightmare he'd had about his father.

"He was screaming that Ian was dead," she remembered, "persistent that he heard Ian calling out to him. He said he heard his father being scared; then, he heard a gunshot. I held him, consoled him, and kept him awake, telling him that it was just a nightmare."

Annie looked up at Susan, the investigators, and Wiley, all staring at her intently, listening with a unified and uninterrupted focus. She looked at the intense expressions on their faces before she spoke, her brown eyes big and wide.

"It was no nightmare," she said, letting it absorb before she continued. "I got Ryan back into bed, and about two hours later, there was a knock at the door. It was the police coming to tell me that Ian had been shot and killed. Apparently, Ian's habit had turned into an uncontrollable addiction, and he'd owed a great deal of money. Late that night, I received a call from someone looking for Ian; the voice was angry, threatening. I hadn't told the police about the mysterious caller that night; I wanted to spare my son, and deep inside of me, I was glad to be finally rid of Ian.

"So, you see, I knew that Ryan was also capable of some type of telepathic ability, just like his father; that was my biggest nightmare. If Ryan had inherited this trait from Ian, who knows what else he may have received. I wasn't willing to find out. I wouldn't let my son be destroyed the way that his father was.

"Then, when the team mentioned that Ryan was clairaudient, and that it was some form of telepathy, that was the only word I needed to hear. What I had hidden from Ryan for his own good was now about to be exposed. I couldn't let that happen."

"And you stopped the sessions?" Susan drew the obvious conclusion.

"Wouldn't you?" Annie said. "I had no one else. What would I do, will I do, without my son?" The tears cascaded down her face once again and this time, the audible sobs came with it, unleashing a desperate plea directed at Wiley. "You have to find him; he's all I've got!"

Susan comforted her as she broke down in her arms.

"Annie, do you understand now what links Ryan to Sidney?" Susan asked, once the sobbing had subsided. "Sidney no longer has any contact with his parents; they don't bother with their son because they are taunted by an unencumbered fear of his ability. Like you, they stopped Sidney's sessions with me many years ago.

"All of these years, they have been unable to accept Sidney for who he is and what he is. Sidney's only family is seated right here." She motioned to the team. "Sidney was an only child; so is Ryan. You only have each other. Keep in mind—it wasn't Sidney who pushed his parents away. They removed themselves from his existence when he was a child—I saw it. They loved their son, just so long as he wasn't what he was, something that contradicted everything they believed in. I know that is not what you want for your son, is it, Annie?"

"Of course that's not what I want for my son," Annie said, with a creaking voice.

"Then you have to make yourself part of this," Susan said. "You have to understand even if you don't want to. If you can't accept it, how will Ryan? I've often wondered if Sidney thinks less of himself because his parents did. You can't let that happen to Ryan. You have to understand, and you have to fight alongside us to get him back."

"Then you have to let me out of here," Annie said. "I will be okay as long as I'm doing something. I want to go home and wait for him, in case he calls or comes ho—" She covered her tearing eyes with her hand, and then composed herself. Just then, Leah walked over to her bedside.

"Annie, I wanted to apologize," she said. "I misjudged you without knowing your whole story. When I first met you and witnessed your response, it made me think of Sidney's parents, and I automatically assumed you belonged in the same category. I'm so sorry for second guessing you. No one should ever use his or her ability to hurt anyone, and I'm sorry for what you went through."

"Hey, don't be sorry," she said, passing it off. "We all misjudge sometimes, and no one has misjudged more than I have. Thank you, Leah. I appreciate it."

They exchanged quick smiles of appreciation, and then Susan announced that she would release Annie the following day, so long as she relaxed and took the mild sedative she was prescribing for her. Then, Wiley spoke again.

"Annie, when you get home, I would like to come over and take a look around Ryan's room, maybe going through his things will give us some hint or clue as to what he knew about Hadley."

Annie agreed, and after Wiley asked, she told him everything that Ryan had mentioned concerning Sidney Pratt. She related how Ryan had been insistent that a girl Sidney was searching for was in trouble, so he tried to communicate with him. Ryan had also known that Sidney was ill, and so he snuck out when she refused to bring him to the hospital.

It all made sense to her now. Dylan and the others revealed to her that Ryan was also capable of hearing the living, even from distances. She had never been aware of this, having removed Ryan from the sessions with them so fast, she failed to learn everything about her son. She had dismissed him when he tried to tell her that he could hear Sidney, and that he could hear things as they were occurring. She should have known that Ryan was like his father. She should have known it when that girl was killed, but like lingering dust, she'd swept it away. It was a mistake she vowed to never make again. All of it was beginning to feel like her fault.

Dylan and Brett also explained to her what Ryan had said when he entered the hospital. He'd heard this Hadley person from a distance and didn't bother to tell her, though it wouldn't have made a difference. Already she felt an overwhelming sense of guilt toward herself, but gratitude toward the team.

"It's time for you to get some rest," Susan said. "I think that's about enough for this evening, don't you, Agent Wiley?"

He agreed just as the text alert on his phone summoned him, and they bid their goodbyes until tomorrow, leaving her alone in her room to think. So Annie laid back, thinking about how she'd failed her son.

* * * *

Wiley sat behind his desk, studying the company name and office address in front of him. He was almost sure that he'd come across the logo at sometime in the past, and if he was right, it matched one of the many false leads once attached to the infamous group the Bureau had been seeking for so many years.

He mentioned this to the team last night after their visit to Annie Quinn. One of the agents at the Bureau had texted him the news that a computer search had resurfaced this once dead lead, yet again, and that it might be worth checking out. Wiley also received other information, and he remembered their conversation outside of Annie's room.

"I didn't want to discuss with her what I'm about to tell you all," he'd said. "It's best for her to gain her strength back. It's not going to do her any good to get upset over something she doesn't need to know yet."

"What is it?" Susan asked, as curiosities peaked.

"I have just received word that Ryan's DNA matched the paper towels on the floor in the men's room. That means that he was snatched from right inside, quickly, professionally, and without a word. My guess is that he was drugged, then hidden in the laundry sack, and carried out of here.

"Also, you all mentioned that you had never seen Hadley, that you didn't even know his whereabouts whenever he contacted you. Is that correct?"

Affirmations were spoken at once.

"But there were times when you thought he was here, in Pennsylvania, correct?"

They agreed, and Brett revealed how once, Sidney thought Hadley might have been stowing somewhere in Pittsburgh.

"That's exactly what I needed to know," he said, retrieving his phone from his inner jacket pocket and showing them the screen. "Do any of you recognize this company name or address in Pittsburgh?"

They all shook their heads.

"I think we may have a lead. I will get back to you on it."

Now in the light of day he stared at the address of what he knew was an office building along Forbes Avenue in Pittsburgh. The address he had never seen before, but when the Bureau came upon the name in the past, MSB Enterprises, it hadn't led anywhere. There was only one way to find out if this company was real or not, and whether it was connected to the rogue group. He was going there to find out.

The search warrant he'd ordered had arrived, and as fast as the courier handed it to him, he was out the door of the headquarters and into his car.

Forbes Avenue stretched a span of ten miles through the heart of the gothic metropolis, and on either side, historic structures stood proudly, jutting out amid the modern ambiance. This drive in particular caused him to admire the famous Cathedral of Learning, the Carnegie Institute, and all the other sites he remembered so well.

He arrived at the section of the avenue where the building would be and then slowed down to search the numbers. The tall business structure shot upward in attempted high-rise glory, and Wiley could see from the sign in the parking lot that a variety of businesses inhabited the structure. He parked the car and entered the building.

The atmosphere was professional, different suites representing different businesses within the private sector. The elevator lifted him up two floors where he needed to go, and soon, the suite number he was searching for almost stared back at him.

He knocked on the door, then waited ten seconds and knocked again.

"Hello," he called out. "Is anyone there?" When he got no response, he twisted the knob gently, and surprisingly, it turned. *Unlocked*, he thought, as he clutched the revolver in his side pocket for safety. He followed protocol when entering, and quickly hit the light switch to expose the darkened room. It was empty, but he called out again, and was greeted by the sound of nothing.

Wiley could tell by the sight of the room that it had been cleared out, abandoned; he'd seen things like this before, scam artists that ran operations, and so forth. The long mahogany desk was clean, no papers, files, no blotter, no artifacts, a barren piece of expensive furniture.

This office had been occupied, and recently; he could tell by the various pieces of furniture that were askew and not even dusty. The visitor's chairs were placed haphazardly, as though someone had not taken the time to place them back correctly. This was not the scene that would be awaiting a new tenant; this was a scene that had been evacuated.

One by one, he pulled open the desk drawers—nothing. That certain someone had also made sure that not even a corner scrap of paper would be left behind, meticulous, yet sloppy. When he got to a bottom drawer, his eye caught a small gadget lying inside. It almost resembled a remote control, only it had two basic buttons on it. He stared curiously at them, wondered what they triggered or opened.

He pressed the first one, and automatically, the window blinds drew forth and closed in a rapid motion, hindering the outside light. He pressed the second button and jumped slightly from the clanking sound behind him. It was a cabinet behind the desk, and the doors drew apart much like the blinds, but this cabinet was inconspicuous, safely misrepresented and concealed by the wall itself. *Now you see it, now you don't*, he thought to himself.

He looked inside the cabinet, and the strangest instinct nagged at him. There was nothing there, but *something* had been there. He kept trying to picture what would have been kept inside it. The answer to that could have been anything. But something had been kept in this cabinet, and it was removed. There was a scratch on the inside wooden surface. This room had been recently occupied; he could feel it. But as his eyes searched around the room, the failure of being too late mocked him in return.

His instincts assured him that the person who had evacuated this private haven was Roman Hadley. That meant only one thing—Hadley was listening...

Chapter Eleven

He'd cleared out of his office as soon he'd picked up the voices. The waning decline of his clairaudient ear became more apparent through the random retrieval of only brief words, like a radio that only received quick blips of reception. It was the FBI, as he knew it would be sooner or later…

"…whereabouts whenever he contacted you?"

"…recognize this company name…Pittsburgh?"

"…have a lead."

He also heard Brett Taylor's voice, revealing that Sidney suspected his whereabouts as being in Pittsburgh. Now, he hoped the clandestine group would respond with a relocation plan; it could make his escape much easier. He knew it would ultimately come to a way out, one way or another.

After hearing the voices, he scrambled to get rid of anything in the office that could connect him to it, including the security monitors that diligently watched the compound, not to mention his guest. He had no immediate choice but to uproot himself to the underground, where a private office, as well as a substantial personal bunker, was always at his disposal. This office certainly didn't equal the fashionable city suite he was used to, but it would suffice.

The time had come for an introduction with his guest. In the night while Ryan was asleep, he had the guards move the large computer screen into the boy's room. He felt a video introduction worked best for their first meeting; it would be easier for the boy to understand and concentrate on what he was telling him.

His laptop sat in front of him; he clicked on the webcam software that would transfer his image to the screen in Ryan's room.

* * * *

He'd awakened in what felt like morning, but he couldn't be sure within these odd surroundings. The air was different, colder, muggier, and the smell that permeated throughout was like clay, wet, and raw. He felt alert now, strangely revived and noticing the scent of almonds had left him. Now, electric lighting filled the room, when during the night, only shades of incandescence glowed softly enough to see.

The nausea that churned his stomach had subsided, after he'd made a few trips to the small bathroom inside of his room. It was equipped with a toilet, shower, mirror, and sink. There weren't any windows in this place, and he wondered why. *Where am I?*, he sat and wondered, ogling something in the room that wasn't there when he awoke during the night.

It was a computer screen, not the personal, portable type, but the kind found in an auditorium, as the ones used during school assemblies. It loomed before his bed, a large, blank square situated on a moveable post, and someone had wheeled it in here while he was asleep, because it wasn't here when he awoke in the wee hours.

It wasn't the only thing he'd found when he woke; there was also a tray on a cart at the foot of his bed. The French toast, bacon, and hash browns told him for a fact that it was morning. He didn't want to eat, eyeing the tray skeptically, apprehensive that it might be drugged or even poisoned; but it certainly didn't smell like it. He tasted tiny bites at first, and the relief his stomach growled caused him to wolf down the remaining breakfast.

He waited. It wasn't drugged, and definitely not poisoned.

Now he stared at the blankness of the screen, wondering what it was for, and suddenly a flash of gray light and a beeping sound brought the screen to life. Lines of static passed quickly to reveal a man's face on the screen. The man was middle-aged with dark hair streaked with gray at his temples.

"Hello, Ryan," he said. "I'm sure you've guessed who I am by now. After all, you've heard me loud and clear with your wondrous ear, haven't you?"

Ryan recognized the voice in an instant. The name of the man he so urgently tried to warn Dylan and the others of lingered on his tongue, but he couldn't think of it. He was slow to remember, trying to gather his thoughts and put them back in the right order.

"Allow me to introduce myself, Ryan. I am Hadley—Roman Hadley. I am your host for the time that you're here. I'm sure we will become fast friends. You see, Ryan, no one is going to hurt you, least of all, me. That is not why you were brought here, and I apologize for the roughness, but there was no other way."

A brief pause passed between them as Ryan thought of what to say.

"What do you want with me?" His lips moved, but he wasn't sure if his voice had come out loud enough.

"I assure you Ryan, no one is going to hurt you," Hadley's voice was dismissive. "You are here so that we may study you, and your ability. You see, Ryan, I am also a clairaudient, like you. I am also aware that you overheard my conversation from a distance. My, what an extreme capability you possess my young friend, and how clumsy am I?"

His laughter, meant to buddy the boy, was lost on him.

"That's the thing, Ryan," Hadley continued. "I never really got the chance to understand my ability; I mean, there were those who studied me, but I never got the opportunity to fully understand my ability at a young age. I had to learn and understand as I went along with it, and soon, I got older. Of course, I came from a different time. So, you see, I'm still learning and finding out.

"You, on the other hand, are being given the chance that I never had. I am giving you the opportunity to fully understand what you have, to be able to utilize it to the best of your ability."

"So, you kidnapped me?"

"It may seem that way to you now, my friend, but you must understand that there are those who still shun people like us. There is still a need to keep our studies hidden. Ryan, if you wanted to explore your ability to its fullest, you would be discouraged, frowned upon, isolated; the rest of the world would react the same way your mother did. I am giving you the chance to fully understand, to master what you have so that it won't control you anymore."

Hadley hit a note as Ryan thought of the voices when he tried to play his video games, coaching him, distracting him, stealing the fun away.

"But you were out to get Sidney, and you couldn't get him, so you took me instead. I heard you!"

"That's not true, Ryan. I have studied Sidney Pratt's ability, but Sidney is limited in his clairaudience; he only hears the dead, not the living, remotely, like you and I do."

"Yes, he can," Ryan protested. "He heard me the night that girl was killed."

Hadley dismissed it with a closing of his eyes and a shaking of his head, though he knew it to be true.

"But not as well as you and I, Ryan," he said. "The thing about us is that our minds are more in touch with our telepathic side. That means you and I are both telepaths. Sidney cannot begin to understand or teach you what you need to know completely. Ryan, Sidney is in the hospital because something triggered inside his brain whenever he had a clairaudient moment. It had caused seizures and later, a cerebral hemorrhage. That is because he is unaware of how to manage and understand what he has."

The outright lie had caused the tears to well up in Ryan's eyes.

"I will help you understand, Ryan. I promise."

"I want my mother! Where is she?"

Hadley assured him that Annie was fine and went on to tell him that he wouldn't be here long, to think of it as a vacation. He would be returned home to his mother, soon.

"When we meet in person, Ryan, very soon, I want you to be comfortable with me. I want you to relax and take a small test of your abilities. It's simple; in fact, you get to rest while you're listening. Then I want you to explain what you heard, the best way you know how. I will see you soon my friend...until then..."

Ryan sat in awe as the screen went blank once again.

* * * *

He sat back in the chair in his bunker and sighed, relieved that part was over. He thought about one of the last things he'd told the boy, about being returned to his mother soon. This double-edged sword worked well in his favor, as the group would assume it was a lie meant for the boy to believe, a catch to keep him complying and hoping. In fact, Ryan *would* be going home, as soon as he could make his break and contact *her*.

She was on the society's board of directors now; she would understand him. She would help Ryan. Whatever happened to him at this point, he didn't care; he just wanted out.

* * * *

Right now, he felt trapped, caged, and almost wild, but the man hadn't been the monster he'd expected. Ryan felt sure that he was not here to help him; he was helping himself in some way. The man said they were going to meet in person, soon. He hoped that meant that he'd be able to leave this room.

Thoughts of his mother, Sidney, as well as his father, ran rampant through his head. He heard his father's voice just before the damp cloth over his mouth snuffed him out, and they grabbed him. There had been silence since then. He listened, engaging with his mind, and the tears burst forth again as he could not hear his father, not since he was brought here.

He continued to reach out to his father, but it was fruitless. He tightened his eyes in fierce determination, concentrating with his soul rather than his mind. In silence, he called out to the one person he knew could hear him...

"Sidney, hear me. Help me! Hadley! Help me!"

Chapter Twelve

Three days had passed since the surgery, and already he felt more like his old self. It was too bad it wasn't enough to let him out of this hospital, but they did move him from ICU to his own room. The bandages were still wrapped around his head, and he lay in the peacefulness of his own room, looking somewhat better than before; the pain in his head had subsided, leaving only a slight numbness to the side of his face. Something drove him out of eons of sleep during the night, this time louder and more real, rousing him from a restful recovery.

He had heard the voice loud and clear... *"Sidney, hear me. Help me! Hadley!"*

The loud mental cry for help was the clapping hand that stirred him in bed, and with a start, he opened his eyes. It was Ryan; what was wrong with him, and why had he mentioned Roman Hadley? He knew something was going on and that they were definitely keeping something from him.

Susan, Dylan, even Leah, all of them acted strangely when they were here, and now it was time for him to find out why. He would ask them to come to his room, immediately. The nurse arrived within seconds of Sidney pressing the call button.

"Tell Dr. Logan and my friends to get here, right now!" Even the troubled look on her face as she turned away told him exactly what he'd already suspected: something had happened while he lingered near death.

* * * *

"He's waiting for us," Susan said, as the team arrived in the hospital lobby.

"And I told you this would happen," Dylan said. "I assure you, he knows."

"Ryan must be calling out to him," Brett said. "Sidney may have heard him. Ryan spoke to him the night of the accident, and he's probably doing it again."

"Don't you all think Agent Wiley should be here?" Leah asked. "He did want to be notified if Sidney mentioned hearing Ryan."

"First, let's find out for ourselves if that is what's happened." Then, Susan relented. "We may as well face it: Sidney is going to have to be told. I, along with Dr. Talbot, was hoping for a little more time, but I guess there isn't any."

Minutes later, they phoned Wiley from Susan's office to tell him what was happening, and from there, walked to Sidney's room. They saw the expression on his face as they entered.

"So, which one of you is going to tell me the truth, because I know something has happened." He stared at them with suspicion, seeing the relief on their faces that he was pulling through, though he was still extremely weak. He wouldn't let them distract him. "Where's Ryan? What has happened?"

Susan said that first, he needed to sit back and relax, that she had to obtain permission from Talbot just to tell him what she was about to tell him. Then, Dylan interceded...

"It should be on us to tell him," he said to Susan. "Let me start from the beginning." She shrugged and sat back.

Dylan told Sidney about how Ryan came to the hospital to see him when he was in surgery, having heard with his clairaudient ear that something was wrong.

"He came into the lounge, adamant that he'd heard a conversation, a plot to kidnap him. He swore that the name he heard was Hadley."

Sidney's face melted at what he was hearing. Dylan continued...

"He said something about Hadley calling him a far more powerful clairaudient than Sidney Pratt, and that he wanted to study him and his ability. When Ryan came here, he was serious, scared; he knew things that he would have no way of knowing, Sid."

"We told Ryan that we would protect him," Brett volunteered. "We failed at that. His mother followed him here, but when Ryan went to the men's room, he was abducted out of this hospital, right under our watch."

Brett's voice wavered and creaked.

"Hadley has disappeared," Leah said. "And we have every reason to believe that he has Ryan, right now.

"It turns out that our friend, Roman Hadley, is part of some underground, psychic rogue group that broke away from the FBI's remote psychic studies years ago. They are committing espionage, and Hadley is the front man; he was never with the FBI. Apparently, he has been listening to you, to us, the whole time, Sid. He has been studying you from afar, hoping that you might be the protégé that was needed for this group, but he discovered the file on Ryan, and he found a better candidate.

"He infiltrated the society to get to *you*, Sidney." Leah's voice was gentle, regretful.

"I know," he said, with a searching stare across his face and a squint of wonder in his eyes. "I don't know how, but somehow, I've always suspected him of something."

Then, Sidney snapped out of his brief pause.

"I have heard Ryan. I heard him last night, and also faintly, the night before. I heard him the night of the accident. That's what I never had a chance to tell you all. It was Ryan's voice I heard, directing me where to go. I couldn't figure it out because something was different about the voice; he wasn't dead. I couldn't identify the voice at first, but then it came to me while I was dreaming, or dying, or whatever it was that was happening to me. You'll never believe where I've been."

He relayed to them all of the scenes he'd endured, telling them about the strange purple sun, then the bright, brilliant luminance that suddenly surrounded him. He told them about his grandfather, and how he called his being there a 'journey,' and that it was not his time. The scenes of his life had flashed by him, as though he was watching a movie, and he described the process in detail, as well as what he saw. He'd seen his life with his parents, the sessions with Susan, the incident in her office, moving to college, meeting and joining the team, but it was hard to recall everything.

He explained that when he woke, he asked for Ryan because Ryan had been *there*, staring at him, and that's when he remembered the boy's name and who he was, realizing that he'd heard a boy that night who was not a spirit.

"Then, Tracy confirmed it for me," he said, waiting for their responses.

"Tracy, Tracy Kimball?" Susan had learned long ago not to doubt

Sidney, but still, her voice remained skeptical.

He told how, as he was about to meet Leah in the parking lot, the pains in his head had become unbearable. He noticed the blood coming from his nose and ears as the static on the main TV screen in Room 208 grew harsh and vociferous. The voice coming from the screen—another pipeline connection and it was Tracy, calling his name. He had no knowledge of what came next, except the blackness, draping down like a stage curtain in the dark.

"I saw her when I was there," he said. "She was with David; they were together, peaceful, happy. She told me that it wasn't my fault, that she had caused what happened to her, just like you said, Susan. She said there was nothing I could have done."

Susan hung on every word, her interest keen and unbroken. Leah was recording with her cell camera, and Brett was taking notes, documenting. All of it would go into Sidney's file because there was the chance that the more time went on, the less Sidney would remember.

"Then she told me about Ryan. She said he was in danger, and that I had to help him. She knew everything, and in life, she didn't even know Ryan." Sidney thought for a moment, his eyes staring off in fatigued curiosity.

"What is it Sidney?" Susan asked.

"There was something else she told me; it was strange. She said to remember the voices that were familiar to me in the journey, to remember what I'd heard, that it was important, somehow."

"What do you think she meant by that?" Susan asked, and Sidney thought for a moment. The look on his face was of someone trying to grasp a dangling object just out of reach. He sighed in exasperation, giving up.

"I don't know," he said. "I can't figure out what it is. It's there, yet it isn't there."

"Well, don't stress on it, now," Susan said. "Talbot would have my head if you had a setback." She eased him backward into the bed, fixing the pillow behind him, making sure he was comfortable.

It was then that Agent Wiley whisked into the room. He nodded to Susan and the others, then stared at the person he had come to see, Sidney Pratt, who looked up at him curiously. Susan quickly made the introductions.

"Agent Wiley, this is Sidney Pratt; Sidney, this is Agent Wiley of the FBI. He is investigating Hadley and conducting the search for Ryan."

"I'm pleased to meet you, Sidney, though under unfortunate circumstances." Wiley spoke quickly, avoiding any delays in what he needed to say. "As Dr. Logan has told you, I am investigating what happened to Ryan Quinn. Now, Sidney, I have read the file on you, kept by your investigative society; I have also read the file on Ryan Quinn. I am familiar with the both of you, the extent of your abilities, and the difference in your abilities.

Wiley assured Sidney of his familiarity in subjects such as clairaudience and remote viewing. He detailed his experience investigating the rogue group, whom he gave Sidney a full explanation of, as well as their activities and intentions. Then, Wiley circled in on his central point.

"Sidney, I need to know, have you been hearing the voice of Ryan Quinn?"

The sound of the question caused all to recognize the magnitude of the situation, instilling an instant, silent shock through the room.

"Yes. I have heard him twice," Sidney said. "His voice was faint the night before, but he kept calling, 'Sidney.' Last night, he spoke more clearly in my mind. I heard him say the name 'Hadley' and the word 'help' a few times. I just finished telling the team that I heard Ryan the night of our friend's accident; he told me in which direction to look for her. He is the only living voice I have ever heard."

Sidney looked at Agent Wiley, wondering if, despite all of his "research," he was able to understand what he was about to tell him, wondering if there was anything that would surprise him.

"Most of the people that I chat with on a daily basis...*are dead*." The slightest hint that Sidney's humor had returned caused hands to quickly hide cracking smiles.

"Tell me about your experience studying Ryan two years ago."

"What you've read is all of it," Sidney said, then proceeded to tell him about the sessions with Ryan. He'd heard the dead much like he had, proving it with concrete details regarding Sidney's grandfather. Then, during a test, Ryan picked up every word the four of them had spoken privately in another room. It was that day they discovered that Ryan had wielded a remote hearing ability with a razor sharp tenacity.

They had concluded that Ryan was also telepathic, and that is what scared Annie, causing her to halt the sessions. Sidney could never manage to get through to her.

"Yes, she explained it all," Wiley said, and Susan filled in the details of Annie's episode when Ryan went missing. Wiley then turned to Sidney and asked him the next question with the sharpness of a reporter. "Did Ryan sound hurt to you in any way?"

"He didn't sound hurt," Sidney said. "He sounded scared."

"That's exactly what I thought." Wiley told Sidney about how the rogue group, and Hadley, was not interested in hurting Ryan, only using him. "That's the one thing that is going to work in our favor, but we have to move fast, especially if I'm right about Hadley, there may be a showdown between him and the group. That would place Ryan right in middle."

"So, let me get this straight, if I may," Sidney said. "Hadley was originally interested in me as a subject, and then when he realized I wasn't telepathic, he went through our files and found Ryan? So, Ryan was chosen in my place?"

Susan sighed at the truth spoken so poignantly, her expression indicating her concern with Sidney's habit of guilt assumption.

"Hadley's focus was to find someone within your group, had it been you, or someone else. I understand that Ryan is a smart kid. Is that correct?"

"Brilliant," Sidney said, the team concurring.

"That may be a problem for us." Wiley's unexpected answer hadn't been considered. What if Ryan resisted, to the point where they couldn't control him? What would they do? When Wiley was confronted with these questions, he offered an unexpected explanation, one by his slight hesitation, he hadn't wanted to give.

"I suspect their method is going to be to brainwash him."

More silence filled the room as the unthinkable began to unfold.

"They might turn him against his mother, the one who tried to suppress his ability, build up his fascination, show him the extent of what he can do; all of which could work."

Wiley quickly changed the subject and moved forward.

"Sidney, what I want you to do, is keep this pad with you." Breaking the silence, he retrieved a small, yellow pad of paper from his inner jacket pocket. I want you to write down every word you hear, if Ryan calls out to you again. I want you to note the time, how long you hear him, how loudly, and any other noises associated with his voice as you are hearing it, understood?"

Sidney agreed, and kept the pad, as well as a pen, on the small, rectangular table that housed his tray next to his bed. Wiley announced that he would be leaving to check some things out. He had a theory that might lead somewhere, if he was right. Not ready to discuss details, he turned to leave.

Susan told Sidney that she would return to check on him in a bit, and the others decided to leave also, saying their goodbyes and leaving their friend to a much needed rest as his eyes began to droop.

He sat drowsing in his bed and breathed a deep sigh as guilt slightly tweaked him.

Chapter Thirteen

Ursula Masters knew that she'd signed on for more than she'd bargained when she realized the extent of the situation. This was not what she had agreed to when she decided to take the dirty, discreet, little job Roman Hadley had offered her. He had come upon her out of nowhere one day as she left the Financial Aid office at the university.

Her tuition was past due for this quarter of the term, and what little money she had left had gone for rent. Financial assistance for students had been waning, while the cost of tuition was rising, and she'd just discovered that she was ineligible for extra assistance, being employed and renting her own apartment.

The frustration of being unable to find a second job had bogged down on the shoulders of the short, plump, young woman in her mid-twenties. Her thoughts turned towards the idea of an under-the-table job, but even with her beautiful violet eyes, flawless face, and black hair, she knew she wasn't the exotic dancer type. She possessed only one profound ability or talent—her clairaudient ear. The man in the limousine seemed to know that when he pulled up alongside her that day...

She strolled out of the FA office, letting the steam blow off her as she walked the campus grounds back to her car, a rickety representation of yet another payment due shortly. Suddenly, her anger and frustration became muted by the appearance of the sleek, black limo that pulled alongside her. *An awesome stretch,* she thought, *must be nice.* The car stopped beside her, and the mirrored window rolled down to her surprise.

"Hello, Miss Masters." The man in the back seat with the silver streaks through his regal black hair had spoken to her. The fact that he knew her name drew her close to an edgy, apprehensive defense mode.

"Excuse me?" She asked with a questioning tone that asked unspoken, 'How the hell do you know me?' She bent down and stared at his handsome face.

"My name, Miss Masters, is Roman Hadley. I am one of the private benefactors of the university. Your situation with FA has come to my attention. I think I may be able to help you, as I have a little proposition for you. Perhaps, you'd like to hear details?"

"Thanks, but I'm not looking for a Sugar Daddy." She turned away to continue on her path, and the car pulled up even further to catch her.

"I assure you, that is not what I had in mind, Miss Masters," he said. "You see, I know that you're clairaudient, so am I. Perhaps you'd like to hear about how your ability can save you financially?"

She hated herself for how quickly she got into the car with a total stranger, but the car pulled into the parking lot of the campus library, so they hadn't gone far. She was also curious as to how he knew about her clairaudience, wondering who on campus was talking about her.

"As I said, Miss Masters, I am also clairaudient, like you," he said, turning to her and smiling. I picked up your thoughts one day, here on campus, when you were thinking about introducing yourself to the university's paranormal investigative society.

She made a slow, swift turn of her head toward him. So, this guy was a mind reader, and maybe a stalker, and here she was in the back seat of a limo with him, again, managing to find herself in the oddest of situations. She felt her desperation steal everything inside of her, leaving her in a state of complete submission.

"What I am in need of, Miss Masters—"

"Look, since I'm crazy enough lately to get into cars with strange people, no offense, I prefer that you just go ahead and call me Ursula."

"Obliged, Ursula," he said. "What I need is a personal assistant, someone to aid in the completion of an assignment that I am now undertaking. You see, I am the coordinator of a highly clandestine and effectively accomplished psychic research society. We research people like you all the time, Ursula. We are providers for those who want to understand more about what they possess psychically. Do you wish to understand it more, Ursula?"

"What's to understand? My sister has it, my mother had it, and her mother had it. I can hear the dead, and can hear conversations over distances. It's a psychic ability that quite a few people around the world possess, more than you know, and I am one of them. I understand, completely."

Hadley laughed at her brash and brassy sense of humor.

"Well said, Ursula. Your job would be quite simple, attending to our subject with whatever is needed. Yes, it would be like being a babysitter, but I assure you, you will be paid handsomely for your work. Should you ever choose to enamor yourself of our expertise by studying your own psychic ability, we would provide you with any assistance as bonus compensation. I could also arrange an introduction with the university's paranormal society when the time comes, if you're still interested.

"Also, your work will not interfere with your class hours; you may come and go freely to accommodate and coordinate your co-existing schedules. Should you choose to accept the position, you will be paid one-thousand dollars in tax-free cash, per day, every day. The remainder of your tuition at this university will be taken care of by the time you reach home, and this, will be your starting wage, a sign of my good faith."

He pulled two folded one-hundred dollar bills from his pocket, flashing them between two fingers. She felt her eyes stuck open wide and staying that way, the fruit from the forbidden tree dangling in front of her. She could probably quit her job at the diner, raking that kind of money in. Her bills would be gone; she could focus on her studies. Her thoughts began to wander.

"There is only one stipulation. As I told you, we are a clandestine research group, and therefore, highly secretive. You must never tell anyone where, or what, you are doing for a living; a cover will be provided for you. We insist upon your silence; it is required."

She stared at the green relief being held out to her. There didn't seem to be any other way, but if he had terms, so did she...

"I don't kill people, and I'm not a prostitute," she said, maintaining her ground. After Hadley assured her that neither was part of her job description, she'd snatched the cash from his hand and was in.

Now she stood outside the tunnel that led to the entrance of the compound he'd described, smoking a Marlboro and regretting her decision. Kidnapping was definitely not what she had agreed to, though Hadley tried to deny that was the situation. He'd become stern and almost threatening when she'd mentioned her concern.

"Do not misinterpret the scenario, Ursula," he said with a slight rise in his voice. "Your only job is to attend to the subject; the boy is our subject. After all, *if* kidnapping were an issue, that would make you an accomplice, now wouldn't it?"

There had been a brief silence between them before he angrily walked away. She was stupefied by what she'd just heard. What had she gotten herself into; how could she have been so stupid? *Psychic research, my ass,* she thought, taking another drag.

She smoked outside the tunnel's entrance, but walked around awhile by the old, abandoned railroad tracks alongside it, not wanting to draw attention to the location. Smoking wasn't permitted within the "compound." *No, smoking? I guess not,* she thought, *it used to be a mining facility.* Something had to be done; she knew that kid had been kidnapped. She was also aware of the need to eradicate her thoughts around Hadley. Her grandmother had taught her that little trick, shutting down her thoughts so no one else could read them. Maybe that's why Hadley was so irritated by her after she took the job; it was harder for him to read her mind.

Right now, she would play it cool and act like she was adapting. She would keep her mind closed and focus on how to get that kid out of here. She wasn't sure what lengths this Hadley guy would go to, and what about this mysterious group to which he'd referred? So far, she hadn't seen anyone other than Hadley, the two security guards, and the kid. Hadley was on the phone all of the time. Maybe this group was always watching...or listening. Her pulse quickened because what she was about to do was risky.

She put the thought out of her head, smothering her cigarette into the dampened ground beneath her with her foot, and walked back to the entrance. It was time to give the kid his tray...

* * * *

This morning, Ryan had awakened earlier, but still failed to catch a glimpse of the person bringing his trays. The only people he actually saw were the two guards and Hadley on the video screen. He sat up on the bed, keeping watch; today was the day he would meet Roman Hadley face to face. He sat and waited for it to happen. This afternoon he would witness, not having slept in, whether it was one of the guards or someone else bringing his trays. He didn't think either of the guards would have left the note he found on his dinner tray last night. He'd taken his first shower in captivity, missing the deliverer of the curious message. It had read simply...

Stay calm! Hide thoughts!

He had already learned to hide his thoughts, yet he kept forgetting. Hadley was older and knew more about this than he did, even picking up a few of his thoughts during the video chat. Now, Ryan couldn't help but wonder if this person bringing his food was also like him, a listener, as Sidney called it. What if this person was a prisoner also?

Other thoughts and questions clouded his mind like why wasn't he hearing his father's voice? What was happening to his mother? Was Sidney awake yet, and what if he wasn't? They had told him that Sidney was going to make it, but a wave of anxiety swept through him when he wondered if he was sending his telepathic SOS's to someone who remained unconscious.

There was nothing to do in this room; he felt like he was going mad. Surely, Hadley didn't expect him to stare at the wall all day long. He was going to show the man the extent of his frustration when he finally saw him. He wasn't afraid of him for some reason, and with that, he felt the slightest edge of the upper hand.

The click of the door caused him to cloak his thoughts, as though he were hiding a forbidden taboo or an unobserved weapon. The roll of the cart came next, and his eyes finally met the person who wheeled it into the room. She was a short girl with black hair, and when she turned, she stopped and stared him straight in the face, saying nothing.

He followed her lead, watching in silence as she brought his lunch over to him. She set the tray on the table next to him and lifted the lid that covered the dish, motioning with her eyes that seemed both dark and light, and somehow, violet. Underneath the lid was another note. Her stare was serious.

"Hope you enjoy your lunch," she said, and covered the dish back with the lid. She turned and wheeled the cart back out of the room, closing the door with a clanking noise behind her. That sound was the door automatically locking, and her eyes met his one last time through its rectangular window.

When she was gone from sight, he sat in front of the small table to eat. One thing he couldn't complain about was the food; his Mom would have been jealous of the cook. He lifted up the lid and grabbed the note, turning his head toward the window to ensure no one was watching. He opened the folded paper and read...

I will get you out of here...soon. Hadley—mind reader! Eat this note!

So, this person was a listener also. Was she working for him? Was she being held too? Who cares, he thought, she's going to help me. He quickly buried the relief he was feeling because if Hadley recognized it, he would suspect. After all, he had to be watching her too.

He downed his lunch quickly, washing it down with the Coke they brought him with every meal. The next part of lunch was certainly not dessert, but it was essential. He tore the note up into tiny pieces, and then chewed them up in his mouth, making spitballs as he did in fourth grade, and then swallowed them one by one.

* * * *

How stupid was she to think that he wasn't watching her, especially after voicing her concerns about kidnapping? How remiss of her not to think of the hidden video cameras placed inside the room to monitor the boy. He had a hard time reading her mind and hearing her thoughts; she was well accomplished in thought cloaking, but he knew she would slip in some way, and she did.

Then again, he should have known that she would never believe the boy was an active and willing participant, there to understand his ability. He naturally assumed that her need for money would overwhelm her moral concerns, but he'd been wrong. She had been feeding the boy notes—literally. Now, Ursula Masters was a weak link he couldn't afford.

The echoing peel of the phone as it rang out through the underground shook him out of his thoughts. He answered the incoming call.

"Yes," he said, knowingly and expectant.

"It is time to meet the boy face to face."

It was one of the few voices he'd answered to over the course of the years. New voices had replaced old ones, and for some time, this one had been a male with a raspy and withered intonation.

"Understood," he said.

"You must induce him to listen into the destinations we proposed. The words and the pictures may coax his ear in the direction we need."

"It will be done, shortly," Hadley answered, squirming nervously in his chair at the words that came next from the unknown authority.

"There isn't much time. The man searching for you and the boy is named Wiley; he is not a fool. Prepare to evacuate if ordered. It has also come to our attention that you have inducted a possible liability into our organization..."

The voice awaited Hadley's response.

So, they had overheard the confrontation after she began asking questions; they were listening. He erased his thoughts before he answered, like wiping away a crowded chalkboard—just in case. Those thoughts were now buried into his soul; after all, they couldn't read his soul.

"Everything is under control," he lied, swallowing hard. "Nothing I can't handle."

"We know you will handle it, should the need to arise."

The beeping sound told Hadley that the conversation was over.

* * * *

There wasn't time to consider Ursula, right now. He had his first face to face meeting with the boy, and the slightest delay would rouse their suspicions. He left his bunker, and walked a short distance to one of the testing rooms, where he would wait for the guards to bring the boy.

The once underground mining facility, revamped by the group years ago, now posed as a subterraneous medical research laboratory. It remained unquestioned as one of the university's various projects in which falsified results of fictional research studies were produced, and no questions were asked. It reeked of earth down here, stale and cold, nothing like the underground facility he'd been subject to in DC, but it served its purpose. What were once noisy, blinking machines were now high-tech computers and scanners, accomplishing the same thing.

The targets that the caller had mentioned were the remote listening points in which he himself had failed. His ability had strongly diminished in the passing years; what used to be remote conversations and fast passing thoughts were now random blips on antiquated radar. What once had been was no more, and he felt the quiet whisperings of the disappointment he presented.

Today, he intended to prove that when he disappeared, the group would have no reservation about placing Ryan at the lead of the operation, with guidance of course. The only change would be that *he* would be gone. He'd considered asking for a trade, a switch, but what if they declined? He would be exposed as a mutineer; they would kill him. There was no other choice but to disappear.

Once he was gone, he would contact her. She would find Ryan, and he would willingly unveil the group. Maybe then mercy would be awarded him, and he could regain some form of his life back, once he explained the last forty years.

But until then, they were listening...

He closed his thoughts and waited for the boy.

* * * *

The guards entered his room, and as usual, he felt no duress, no intimidation from them. In fact, they were friendly, but he suspected that had something to with his age. He recalled his teacher's explanation of the phrase "kid gloves," when they came to bring him to the testing room, as though they were taking him to school.

"Mr. Hadley wants to sit and talk with you, Ryan." The older of the two guards had spoken—odd, because they didn't speak much.

His heart raced, awakened by the inevitable invitation. He stood and put on his shoes, then looked up at the guards, ready. They walked him down the spacious corridor, his eyes catching sight of endless doors to the left and to the right. He realized that the rooms were where subjects were examined, and abilities were tested, and experiments were conducted. Even though the guards allowed him to walk in front of them, that's exactly what he felt like right now, a subject to be examined, pointed at, studied as though he were some inexplicable microcosm.

Ahead, he noticed a room where the light inside spilled out into the corridor more than the others. That was where he was going, and inside, he heard a man clearing his throat and breathing meditatively to catch his nervous breath. It was Hadley; he could hear him. He stopped in front of the room and turned to the guards, allowing them to open the door and escort him in.

The room was basic, devoid of furniture except a desk and chair, a recliner, and a tall filing cabinet. The once decrepit walls still depicted cracks and scars that snuck through the painted white. The man he'd met on the video screen slowly raised his head, and their eyes met each other's in subdued fascination.

"Hello, Ryan," Hadley said. "You know who I am. Please have a seat."

Ryan sat on the opposite side of the desk from his captor, feeling the blank stare of his face hardening into a mask. After Hadley inquired about the accommodations, he complained about the restless tedium he felt inside the room, with no television, books, or video games.

"We may be able to rectify that situation as your productivity increases," Hadley said. "Remember, Ryan, your main focus now is honing your ability. You have something that not many others possess. It is a gift."

Ryan understood what he meant; the more information he was able to feed him, the more activities he would be allowed.

"I want to talk to Sidney," he said, adamantly.

"I'm afraid that is impossible, but you should know that our friend, Sidney, is doing just fine. I'm sure you've found it hard to communicate with him because first, Sidney is not a telepath, and secondly, his ability may be in jeopardy due to the trauma he suffered."

A nagging knowledge from the pit of his stomach told Ryan that this was untrue, but he tried not to contest Hadley, feeling the need to play along, allow him to think he was in control. He definitely didn't fear the man; there was something about him that made him unable to do so. Ryan couldn't identify it; it was as though fear and pressure lived beneath the man's exterior.

"As I was saying, you are unique, Ryan. Society shuns what you have because they don't possess it themselves. Why do you think your mother was stringent about your not using your ability? She tried to suppress it in you because you're capable of communicating with your father, something she doesn't want."

That last comment stole him away from his inner focus, and silently, he wondered if it was true. He'd always felt that there were problems between Mom and Dad, because he'd heard them fighting off and on, but they were problems he didn't *see*. He'd ignored it all, hoping it would go away...but not the way it had. He'd soon forgotten about it, never mentioning a word to his mother.

"You must use this time, Ryan, to strengthen your ability, use it to help people. You can only learn how to do that, here."

Ryan's mind wandered, juggling in the circus of thoughts that Hadley's words induced into his mind.

* * * *

He was fully aware of Ryan's capabilities, and therefore didn't waste too much time testing them. He coaxed Ryan into listening to the conversation the guards were having in another part of the underground. The boy closed his eyes, shut himself down to everything around him, and reached out with his mind—astounding.

When Hadley called the guards in, Ryan repeated their conversation, verbatim, producing reactions of tense amazement and proving himself to be of the highest caliber of clairaudients. Hadley stared at this prodigy whose ability had dwarfed his own.

"Ryan, tell me about your ability to hear the dead," he said.

Ryan described for him the deafness, then the sound of the dead person's voice, almost like an echo. All of it was familiar to Hadley; he had possessed the same abilities since his own childhood. He explained to Ryan how remote hearing meant that his telepathic side was just as powerful as his ear to hear the dead.

Then he saw the look of distraction on the boy's face, the far away stare of his deep green eyes, as though he were listening. Hadley tried to glean what was happening, but was unable. The voices of the dead that spoke to him at one time had long maintained their silence toward the cause of Roman Hadley. This was why Ryan would be a much greater asset.

"Ryan," he said. "What are you hearing?"

The boy casually turned his head to him, seemingly broken from a spell.

"Nothing," he said, but Hadley felt the grip of his upper hand slowly slipping away.

* * * *

Ryan sat back in his room, silently overwhelmed by the rush of relief that surged inside him, not only because the session with Hadley was over, but because he had finally heard his father's voice during it. His captor had been interviewing him regarding the dead that spoke to him, and it happened. No longer could he hear Hadley's words as the deafness erased all sound, and Hadley's lips had continued to move in endless unheard speech.

"Ryan, stay calm. They're coming for you, soon."

He relied on hearing his father, and he wondered why it had been days, right when he needed him most. Though he didn't fear Hadley, the situation had knotted a lump of anxiety in the middle of his chest that burst and dissolved at the familiar voice. He had looked away from Hadley, and then quickly tried to hide the change in his demeanor.

"I will get you out of here, son."

The words were fast and fleeting, then gone, and suddenly he heard

Hadley asking him what he'd heard. Nothing, he'd told him, and he seemed to believe it. Obviously, Hadley hadn't been lying when he described his own ability as having dissipated, or he would be listening himself. He had just failed at hearing the words of Ryan's father.

Next, he was talking about listening to certain destinations. He instructed Ryan to sit back and relax, so he was now stretched out on the recliner. Then, Hadley showed him a few pictures. The first was easily recognizable.

"Ryan, this is The White House," Hadley said, holding the picture. "Listen..."

Something about the smooth, strange, coaxing way Hadley said the word caused him to comply. The sounds from elsewhere took over...

"Mr. President...press conference...deputy...organizations..."

The words and the voices overwhelmed each other as many varied tones spoke out amid the unseen gathering of constructive confusion. He repeated what little he'd heard, explaining that sometimes, what he heard presented itself.

Hadley showed him other photos: the UN building, the capital building, as well as destinations along the US border. All of what he'd heard was varied and jumbled: voices, words, or nothing at all in some cases. The enthusiasm in Hadley's face earlier seemed to be missing now as the wrinkles in his forehead made him look confused.

"You've done well for your first session, Ryan," he said. "We will try harder next time, reach farther, try to search for important conversations."

Now Ryan lay back in his room, almost sleepy, focusing again to reach out to Sidney. He thought of his father watching over him, knowing what he'd said was the truth; they would be coming for him, soon. The lifted burden from his shoulders caused him to slip away into much needed sleep.

Chapter Fourteen

The voices of the conversation came abruptly to her ear. It had always been that way when a distant conversation was about her. She would hear it, as though some guardian angel had intended her to. Now, that angel seemed to be by her side.

"...come to our attention that you've brought a possible liability into our organization."

"Nothing I can't handle..."

"...handle it, should the need present itself."

The voices belonged to Hadley, and some mysterious cohort, probably part of the group that he mentioned. They were talking about her; she knew it whenever her nerves fluttered, and she shuddered inside from what felt like her stomach dropping.

They spoke about killing her; Hadley must have found out about the notes.

She had to flee this place before the guards or Hadley saw her...or anyone else who may have been watching. She would think of some other way to help the kid once she took off in the car. The scattered gravel from the retired railroad tracks crunched louder under her feet the faster she moved. Her light blue VW loomed closer and closer in the small, off to the side, parking area.

When she reached it, she slammed the door shut, automatically locking it. Her breath was heavy, rasping; she had to quit smoking. The engine regurgitated as usual when she keyed the ignition. *Not now,* she thought, *I don't need this.*

"Come on, you piece-a-shit!" She yelled through the small car, the engine ironically purring to life at the sound of her angry voice. It took her mere seconds to leave the remote, desolate part of town behind in a cloud of its own dust.

The farther away she drove, the more the mist in her head began to clear, and she could think of her next logical move. Thoughts ordered themselves into proper sequence, and she remembered something—a name. Just before they mentioned her, the ominous voice mentioned someone searching for the boy.

Wiley...Wiley...not a fool...

Wiley, she knew that name. In fact, there was a guy she waited on often in the diner who was rumored to be FBI. Ed, the owner, always referred to him as "The G-Man;" she always referred to him as "Mr. Wiley." Could it be the same person? It made sense. She would take the risk, drive to the diner and find out. Thankfully, she hadn't quit her job just yet. If Wiley was FBI, she was going to need him on her side, once she explained.

A maroon-colored Sedan appeared in the rearview mirror out of nowhere; it seemed to be trailing her. She stepped on the gas lightly, shifting her eyes from the road to the mirror, but the Sedan continued to follow her.

* * * *

Stu Wiley had a habit of trusting his intuition and being right almost every time. He hinted to the others that he might have a lead, but vocally distributing information, especially in public, was out of the question in this case. The Bureau had been searching for and following this group for years, but their capabilities were immense and far-reaching, achieving feats of espionage through a conglomeration of highly sophisticated psychic beings. That was how they managed to elude authorities for so many years...they listened.

He thought back to the discovery of the underground tunnel back in DC. The group had exhausted quite a few locations, and Wiley knew that the nation's capital would be next to impossible for them to hibernate in, in the current day and age. He felt sure this time that the theory of Hadley being anywhere in the world was nothing more than a cat and mouse game, a wild goose chase, but any number of clichéd sayings would fit the theory he was now ready to dispel.

The signature style of "in plain sight," or "right under the radar of the authorities," was how Hadley and the group had operated throughout the years; it was a repetitive pattern maintained in many different ways from using the FBI as a cover, to the tunnel in DC back in the seventies, and now to the university's investigative team.

It suddenly occurred to Wiley like the appearance of a lost object; what if Hadley and the group were functioning here, right amid the continuous humdrum of the small, Pennsylvania town? Sidney Pratt had suspected Hadley of being nearby in Pittsburgh. What if he was closer than that? Wiley thought.

He'd retrieved official blueprints of the entire county, combing with fine detail any underground locations: mines, waste facilities, anything that could be renovated to match the site in DC. There were many mining facilities in Pennsylvania, most in functioning utilization—those were of no interest to him.

There was one defunct mining facility situated amid a vast underground, and it was only ten minutes from where he sat. He knew of these mines from when he was a kid, but was never really sure what became of them. Could it be possible that Hadley could be so close? *Why not? He had to get to Ryan somehow.* What would make him remain here after taking the boy? It had to be more than just the use of the signature style.

It took him only minutes on his laptop to discover that those old mines had been renovated into a medical research facility. He felt warmer; now all he had to do was discover the sponsor of the medical research, probably another dummy company used as a cover for the group, or what if the facility itself was a dummy headquarters? He stared at the blueprints, his inner instinct swelling a surge through his body. It had to be, but if Hadley was there, it meant something was keeping him here, but what?

Silently, he felt like a lottery winner, and then the phone rang.

Surprised to see Ed's Diner on his caller id, he answered it. It was Ed who nearly shouted in his ear...

"Hey, Stu, one of my girls here says she needs to see you. I'm not sure what she's talking about, something about a missing boy or—"

Another voice interrupted Ed's, as though the phone had been pulled away from him.

"Mr. Wiley, this is Ursula Masters. I've served you several times in here—dark haired waitress? Are you the one looking for the boy, Ryan?"

Wiley knew her, but the surprise of what she uttered stunned him speechless.

"If so, I know where he is, but you have to come now, I think someone has followed me."

* * * *

"Whatever it is, it's like it's calling me back there." Leah heaved a distressing sigh, lounging back in the comfortable chair in Susan's office. They were continuing their earlier discussion of her recurring visions, while Dylan and Brett were visiting Sidney.

"I keep seeing the scenes of my life in that house over and over: the rocking chair, the spun spool of yarn that I followed down the hallway, Agnes, the basement, my mother. The scenes flash before me, faster and faster, like there's a message I haven't received."

"And you continue to see things you didn't see at the time, like your mother hanging, your father being strapped in a straight-jacket?" Susan had known this, and her point was that of confirmation.

Leah nodded, wiping away a perfect sized teardrop from her eye.

"Is there anything different about the scenes each time? You said you thought there might be a message?"

Leah recalled the visions, especially the last one; there was something different.

"The couple of times when the visions came to me in my dreams, I could hear breathing, a rapid, harsh, almost muffled breath. I kept moving closer and closer to the large, Victorian mirror that my mother had ordered me not to go near. I finally came upon it and looked, and this hideous face stared back at me. It wasn't like anything I had ever seen before; it didn't look human. It was distorted, mutated, and horribly grotesque."

Leah conjured the first words she could think of to describe what stared back at her in the mirror just before she woke from the dreams that accentuated the horrid visions.

"That part never happened in my life," she said. "I never got close to the mirror. It was a gigantic oval glass, so my mother was insistent that I not go near it.

"Leah, what are the early impressions that you have of your mother that linger with you today? What kind of a person did you see her as?"

Leah thought back to her mother, and how she and her father were two completely different people. Her memories of her were few.

"She was pushy, strict, but not really mean, just...selfish, now that I look back. I have always wondered why she married my father when she was so career oriented."

140

"Leah, it could be that—"

Suddenly, the room was enveloped in a mist, and Leah saw a man jump out from behind Susan, who sat behind her desk, talking on, and blind to what Leah was seeing. Leah sat across from Susan's desk, seeing the man in full view as he stepped closer and stood directly behind Susan.

Susan reacted to Leah's unblinking eyes and parted lips.

"Leah, what's wrong?"

Leah didn't answer, only stared behind her.

"My God," Susan said, jumping up from the chair.

"What are you seeing?"

"There's a man behind you, Susan," she said, pointing with her finger.

Susan turned and saw nothing, then stepped aside. The tall, structured man with reddish brown hair stared at Leah, having come to approach the seer. Unlike so many spirits she had seen, this one spoke inside her mind.

"Leah, I am Ian, Ryan's father."

The surprise when she told Susan whom she was seeing made them forget Cedar Manor. Leah leapt from the chair, facing the spirit and obtaining her position of control.

"Look," he said, then pointed to his left. She looked to where he was pointing, and then through the mist appeared an entranceway, a tunnel, a set of old railroad tracks.

"Ryan," he said, continuing to point. Then she caught a glimpse of Ryan, sitting on a bed in a room. Quickly, another face came and faded amid the mist, a man with dark hair and gray at the temples.

"Hadley," he said, the words forming in her mind.

It was the first time she had seen Roman Hadley. The tracks, those old railroad tracks looked familiar. She continued to stare at the sight until the mist evaporated and Ian was gone, as though he never was there, and the room resumed as unbroken.

"Leah, talk to me," Susan asked in a now calmer tone. "Is he still there?"

Leah turned to face her, eye to eye.

"I think I know where Ryan is."

* * * *

Sidney sat up in bed as Dylan and Brett had just left his room. Dr.

Talbot had called his rate of recovery astounding, but continued to warn against stress. That is why Sidney didn't tell him what he had just told Dylan and Brett, that he was still hearing Ryan...

"Without getting upset, Sid, what has Ryan said?" Dylan had asked the question calmly with Sidney understanding that it was crucial to finding Ryan.

"He keeps calling my name," Sidney said. "He mentions Hadley, but nothing else. I'm not so sure he understands or knows where he is. There was one other word he mentioned: testing."

"Hadley is obviously testing the extent of his abilities," Brett said.

"Yeah, but where? Sid, we are going to come back tonight in case you hear anything else. In the meantime, we have to tell this to Agent Wiley, after we retrieve Leah from Susan's office." Dylan stepped backwards to the door as he spoke.

Sidney looked up curiously.

"What's wrong?"

"Nothing, she's fine," Dylan said, as he and Brett left the room.

Now, Sidney couldn't help but recall Tracy's ominous words that the voices he'd heard in the journey would be familiar for a reason. It was a clue, something that he was subconsciously aware of, but had inadvertently buried. He thought back to everything he'd seen during the journey, but it was the episode inside Susan's office when he was a boy that kept coming back to him like a boomerang.

What was so specific about that day? He thought about Mark, the lost love of Susan's life. He heard the voice again in his memory...

"Call her Suzy Q; and tell her that Mark loves her..."

He kept hearing it over and over, and something was not only familiar, but significant about that voice. He hadn't realized it before, but the voice was like Ryan's, which would mean...*the voice was alive, not dead!*

How could it be? Susan mentioned Mark being killed in Vietnam. Was it possible that he was still alive? But if Mark was alive, like Ryan had been, why was his voice so acutely familiar? He hadn't heard it since that day—or had he?

Mark's voice repeated in his mind, and then suddenly he heard the same voice in a different context, using words he'd heard spoken to him before...

"I can't begin to tell you, Sidney, how impressed I am with the

team's research and accomplishments. Keep up the good work..."

Then the dialogue of a more recent instance interrupted.

"I am truly sorry for the loss of Tracy Kimball, Sidney. You all did the best you could...no one is to blame..."

The different words, spoken by the same voice, jumbled together.

"Suzy Q...can't begin to tell you...Tracy Kimball..."

Sidney felt something like electricity flow through him at the realization that was dawning, a revelation that came to him in the peaceful, quiet confines of his room. It can't be, he thought, but the voices of Mark and Roman Hadley were undeniably the same!

The heat of panic started to stifle him, and he exhaled in a long, dramatic release. He had to do something, learning by now to trust his intuitions. It didn't matter if he was wrong. Ryan's life was at stake, but if Roman Hadley and Mark was the same person, he had to tell Susan first...

Chapter Fifteen

Ursula's eye peeked covertly from behind the curtain that draped the diner's picture window overlooking the parking lot. She scanned with caution as far as her eye could see, but failed to see the maroon Sedan anywhere. She pulled her craning head away from the window as Ed trudged back in from outside.

"There's no maroon Sedan out there, Ursie," he said. "You wanna tell me what you got yourself wrapped up in now, or do I have to clear all of my customers out of here? Have you been freaking people out again, like that time you repeated that couple's private conversation about you to their faces?"

She hadn't liked their comments about her, thinking back. They'd been rude, saying she was slow, which she wasn't, and whispered opinions on how it was a shame that her ass didn't match her face as far as assets went. Before giving them their check, she showed them the extent of what she could do, even if she had been all the way in the kitchen. They'd left without paying.

She sighed before she answered, wishing this dilemma would equal by comparison.

"No, Ed, but I think there may be trouble," she said, assuring him not to call the police, that Wiley was on his way over.

Ed stared at her silently, then ran over to the window and gazed out—no Sedan.

"Doesn't look like anyone followed you," he said, but she knew that Sedan was right behind her when she turned for the parking lot. It had to be waiting...somewhere.

Ed looked behind him, relieved that no one was staring, and escorted her to his office.

"I want you to wait for Wiley in here," he said. "If someone did follow you, I don't want any trouble, Ursula."

She agreed and sat in his office, waiting, thinking on how much of a target she had been for Hadley. She hadn't realized, at first that the man was a telepath, capable of getting inside people's minds. He had telepathically sniffed out her interest in the paranormal society, after he, a complete stranger, listened to her thoughts. He then sought her out as another clairaudient, expecting to use her to help him commit a criminal act.

The money had dangled in front of her, and she had snatched it out of his hands as though it were Halloween candy. How stupid, gullible, and desperate she had been. Now her only hope was that she could lead Wiley to the kid, and explain that she had no idea; then maybe, they wouldn't charge her as an accessory...

* * * *

Wiley couldn't believe the phone call he'd received moments ago. The waitress down at Ed's knew where to find Ryan Quinn; how the hell was that possible? He knew who she was; she'd waited on him most of the time, since he usually sat at his preferred table if available. He always forgot her name—Ursula. So, how the hell does a young girl like Ursula get mixed up in this?

But he was elated at what she had told him. If it were true, he might even be able to get Ryan home, where he belonged, today. What if today was the day that after all these years, the Bureau would finally crack this group? And it would all be because of the quiet young waitress named Ursula, who poured his coffee and served him BLT's.

Incredible, but he knew something was about to break; though he had to move fast, silently admitting to himself that if Ursula was right, and she was followed, she might just disappear before he got there. He was hurriedly throwing his coat on and gathering the blueprints from his desk, deciding to bring them to the diner. First, he would sit with Ursula and listen to her story, and then he would call for backup so she could lead him there. He was about to leave his office when his cell phone rang; it was Leah Leeds.

He answered then stopped in his tracks when she spoke...

"Agent Wiley, I may know where to find Ryan!"

"What?" Wiley stopped and stared, stumped and listening to the uncanny.

"I've seen Ian Quinn, tonight, here in Dr. Logan's office."

He remembered that the young woman he was speaking to was a seer, a medium of sorts, saw the dead like Pratt heard them. The reaction of being pressed for time was dispelled as he pulled an extra chair beneath him and sat.

"He showed me an entranceway, a tunnel-like structure down by the old railroad tracks. I remember those tracks from when I was a kid; they're retired now, and they run through the old mining part of town. I heard there is some kind of underground facility somewhere near there, today."

Wiley remembered from childhood also. His instinct had been right again, right here in town, not in plain sight, but underground. He knew it.

"Leah, I want you to listen," he said. "I just received a call from someone who may also know where Ryan is, hopefully because she's seen him. I'm to meet her at Ed's Diner, now. Would you, Dr. Logan, and the team meet me there?"

Leah anxiously agreed, and as the call ended, Wiley was out the door.

* * * *

Dylan and Brett arrived outside of Susan's office, meeting the two women as they were leaving in haste. Leah described for them what had taken place only minutes before.

"Wiley wants to meet us all at the diner," Susan said. "We were just coming to get you. There's no time to fill Sidney in, right now. Let's wait and see what happens."

"We can all go in the van," Dylan said. "I'll drive."

They were on their way to the elevators when a nurse met them in the corridor.

"Dr. Logan," she said. "Sidney Pratt wants to see you, now. He says it's urgent."

"Right now?" Susan said. "Tell him I will be in to see him as soon as I get back."

"I'm afraid he's not going to like that, Doctor. He told me to make sure you didn't leave the hospital without seeing him." The nurse's tone implied that her patient was in need to see the shrink, which worked on Susan, who sighed in frustration.

"Damn! All right, I'm coming," she said, then turned to the team. "You're all going to have to go without me. I'll meet you all when I get there, and tell Wiley that I won't be long, that it concerns Sidney."

Brett offered to stay and ride along with her, to which she declined, and then the investigators disappeared behind the elevator doors. Susan walked to Sidney's room, the concern and wonder etched upon her face.

He looked up at her when she entered, but it was concern on his face that stared back at her.

"What's wrong?" She asked, as he motioned her to the chair by his bedside.

He asked where the others were, hoping for privacy, and his eyebrows rose when she explained everything to him.

"So, you picked an odd time to see me," she said. "I was about to leave with them. Wiley asked that I be there."

"I think you need to be here," he said. "There's something we need to discuss."

Sidney detailed more about the journey and Tracy's words, of which she'd already known what little he'd told previously.

"I wanted to ask you to tell me more about Mark," he said.

"Mark?" She asked, taken aback. "Sidney, you called me back here at the most crucial time to ask me about Mark?"

"This is important," he said. "You wouldn't be sitting here if it weren't."

"What do you want to know?"

"Mark was a listener wasn't he?" Her eyes shifted to the floor, her silence serving as the answer he'd already figured. "That explains why you were so eager, so focused on studying me when I was a kid. It was not my ability that stirred your interest in parapsychology; it was Mark's. When he spoke to me that day in your office, I reconnected you to him."

"Yes, you did," she said. "And yes, he was a clairaudient. I never had the chance to tell you that, Sidney, since everything that happened to Tracy, then to you..."

"I know," he said. "You must have been absolutely devastated when he was killed." Something about the way Sidney spoke told her that he'd arrived at his reason for asking these questions, as though he were fishing for info. She glanced over at him.

"I never said he was killed, Sidney," she said. "He was reported as MIA for many years, over the course of which, I *assumed* he was killed, especially after you heard him. And after forty-some odd years..."

Fear overshadowed Sidney's eyes like a darkening eclipse, and the straightforward stare of his rounded orbs alarmed and interrupted her.

"Sidney, what is it?"

* * * *

He wasn't sure how he was going to tell her what he had to tell her, but he felt almost positive that Mark was Roman Hadley. If it was true, Susan could stop all of this and see to it that Ryan came home.

"When I saw the visions as I was dying, that moment in your office was one of the events in my life that was played out over again, very distinctly. It was as if I was *living* it all over again. I heard Mark's voice, just as I had that day. And Susan, I realized that his voice was familiar to me, not at the time it happened, but later, as though I'd heard it again in my life."

She stared at him with confusion that made him want to tell her faster; he sighed and lowered his head for a moment to think.

"The voice kept playing over and over to me. I did hear that voice again in my life, but I never identified it. I had only heard Mark one time and only a few words. Tracy told me during the journey that I would figure it out, and I have."

She leaned in closer to him, hell bent to hear what he would say.

"Susan, the voice of Mark is the same as Roman Hadley's."

The poise of her face sank as tense muscles melted away. She watched him, speechlessly unnerved.

"When I heard Ryan's voice; it was different. That's when I realized that Ryan was alive, that I'd heard a living person from a distance. I had never done that before, at least, I thought I hadn't. In my life, I'd only heard the dead, until the night I heard Ryan. I didn't realize there was another time, long before that one. The Mark that I heard in your office was alive, just like Ryan; I know that now. His voice is the same as Roman Hadley's."

He watched her slowly rise from the chair with her face lost in frozen confusion, a look of sneaking, silent, fleeting madness.

"Do you have any idea what you're saying?"

The words slipped from her in slow gasps of astonishment.

"He has been dead for years! There is no way, no way in Hell that he would have gone all this time without contacting me! Mark could never, never—"

"Susan, please trust me," he interrupted. "You have to find Ryan because I can't leave here. You have to be objective; you are now the one who holds the key. You have to figure this out! If I'm wrong, I will forever apologize to you, but I'm not, and I don't think you believe I am, either."

She stood at the foot of his bed, weakened in helpless abandon. Denial, shock, and her widened eyes and quivering lips displayed the hurt he knew was twisting inside her.

"Susan, please wake up. Do something! You have to save Ryan. Go find Mark, but please be careful."

The pleading sound of his voice and the hurt he felt for her right now made him realize how much this woman meant to him.

"Go, Susan, now, before it's too late!"

The tears streamed down her face as she turned and ran from his room.

He wept for her, but he knew she would be all right. Susan Logan was tough.

Chapter Sixteen

Ed was waiting for Wiley, and as soon as he walked through the door, he led him back to his small office where Ursula was waiting. The young waitress that he remembered well lowered her head in relief at the sight of him. Wiley assured them that unmarked, undercover agents were surrounding the diner in different locations, incase Ursula had been followed. Ed left them alone in his office.

"Now, Ursula, let's start from the beginning," he said. "You said that you know where Ryan Quinn is, correct?"

She was nodding her head before he ever finished the question.

"I didn't know, I swear to God, I didn't!"

"Okay, okay," he said, calming her, "like I said...from the beginning. I think we can help each other, here, Ursula. You need to trust me, right now, all right?"

She nodded her head again and took a deep breath.

"I am a clairaudient, Agent Wiley," she said. "I have been for most of my life; it is an inherited trait that runs wild in my family. I attend the university, and for a while, I'd been thinking of inquiring into its paranormal investigative society. It was something I kept putting off, you know—I felt really weird about it, about myself, and my ability. One day last week, I almost stopped there, but I passed it up, walked to my car, and left.

"Then a few days later, this limousine approached me as I was walking on campus, and this guy—he knew about me, knew what I could do, knew about my thoughts. To make a long story short, he offered me money to be part of what he called 'psychic' or 'paranormal' research, something or other. He was a clairaudient also, and he spooked me when I realized that, that day, he'd heard my thoughts about approaching the society, as if he was listening, watching.

"But still, I was desperate for the money. I agreed, but I swear I had no idea what he was really doing."

"You're doing great, Ursula," he said. "Look, I know this guy you're talking about. His name is Roman Hadley; am I right?"

Her mouth opened in a mixture of surprise and relief.

"So, you know?"

"We've been tracking him and his group for years, and Ursula, you are the first known person to have seen Roman Hadley; you should be extremely proud of yourself."

"He introduced himself as one of the university's benefactors," she said, then went on to describe him after Wiley asked. "Medium height, dark hair with streaks of gray at the temples, you know, salt and pepper, dark eyes, handsome man, actually, but creepy, very creepy."

She went on to detail how she was instructed to attend to the subject; one of her duties was bringing him his tray. She'd assumed that the subject was a grown man, having entered the research facility on a voluntary basis, until she discovered that it was a boy of about twelve. Yesterday, she'd realized that the boy had been kidnapped and that Hadley was, in fact, a telepath.

"When I confronted him, he threatened to make me look like an accomplice."

She told how she'd decided to try to rescue Ryan, as well as herself, from the underground nightmare; she described the notes, then the phone calls from people who she'd assumed were his superiors, and how Hadley started to become nervous.

"That's what I want to know, Ursula. Did you ever see anyone else there, while you were there?"

"No," she said, shaking her head and needing no time to think. "Only the two guards, Hadley, and the boy."

"Only two guards?" He asked, incredulously. "You never saw anyone else there? Anyone ever come to the compound, maybe someone you've forgotten?"

"Nope, those guards were the only ones that I saw. No one ever came there, but Hadley did speak on the phone several times. It was after one of his conversations that..." She took a deep breath as she broke off, then her voice began to quiver. "I heard bits of a whispered conversation, remotely, that is. It was Hadley's voice, and another man's; they were talking about me, about how I would have to be dealt with. I got away from there, as fast as possible, and that's when I came here and had Ed call you. I saw a maroon-colored Sedan following me before I even got out of that part of town. It was close behind when I turned into the lot, but now it's not out there."

Then Ursula pointed out the location on the blueprints that he showed her.

"Ursula, you did great, and I assure you, with your help in finding Ryan, no one is going to charge you. You're a victim here; we know that."

She looked as though at least a half a ton of weight had been lifted from her shoulders, leaving an uncertain other half to remain.

Just then, Ed opened the door, showing Leah, Brett, and Dylan into his office.

* * * *

Wiley introduced them though no introductions were needed for her benefit; Ursula was well familiar with who they were.

"There isn't time to discuss details, not now," Wiley said. "But Ursula knows where Ryan is, as well as Hadley. She's going to lead me and my backup there."

"I know where he is also," Leah said, describing in detail the incident in Susan's office and confirming the description of Hadley that Ursula gave.

"Okay," Wiley said. "I want you two girls to stick together, so you both can ride with me. Guys, this could be dangerous, so I want you to stay safe and some distance behind my backup when we're on the road.

"From what Ursula has told me, there were only two guards at all times in the compound. My backup is going to storm the place as soon as Ursula directs them where to go. Then, I want you girls to stay as close to me as possible—got it? Like I said, this could be dangerous; we are unsure what to expect. I want you all to remain alert, and guys, I want you parked behind the backup vehicles when we get there, waiting for the girls when I send them back out.

"By the way," Wiley said, looking around, having missed a certain absence. "Where is Dr. Logan, I thought she was going to be here?"

"She needed to stay behind with Sidney," Dylan said. "We aren't sure what the issue was, but he wanted to see her."

"Just as well," Wiley said. "Let's just hope that issue wasn't about

Ryan."

Then he rolled out the blueprints and pointed to the spot that Ursula had shown him, going over quick instructions and order of procedure.

"Let's do this quickly, silently, and pray no one gets hurt. Remember, the FBI is in charge here. When I tell you to stay close, or move away, or get back to your vehicles, you do it, understand?"

Issuing his final instruction, Wiley radioed his backup before leaving the office, and then the four of them calmly walked out of the diner, careful not to rouse attention.

* * * *

The maroon-colored Sedan sat in an alleyway a hundred yards north of the small diner, perched high atop a winding hill that provided a bird's eye view of the location. The well-trained eye of the unknown driver noticed two distinct cars park in two different directions of the diner, conspicuously, as neither driver exited the vehicles.

"Unmarked?" The equally mysterious passenger asked.

"Definitely unmarked," the driver replied.

"The agent is now leaving with the girl. We must leave here, quickly but casually. It is over; our time at this location is up. If Hadley is to survive, he must evacuate now."

The passenger retrieved a cell phone from the inner jacket pocket of his black suit, and pressed a single speed-dial button.

* * * *

Hadley was becoming antsy, pacing and fidgeting at the feeling that stirred inside him, like time was running out. He felt like there was no need to go through the same cycle over again with the boy, poking and prodding, hoping to extract the tiniest piece of information that would satisfy the others. His only intention now was to obtain the information from Ryan that was vital to his plan; where was Susan Logan, right now? Hadley had searched, listened with his own clairaudient ear, and failed.

He also planned to discover whether or not Ryan was capable of that same strange ability that he, himself, had stumbled upon while in Foster's captivity, the act of telepathic intrusion. He remembered well how he gazed into Caleb's mind, picturing his thoughts and stealing his mental images while the Herculean brute fought hard against the invisible intruder. Caleb lacked the mental capacity to fight what he knew was happening, and so a seizure caused his hemorrhaging brain to collapse and expire. Sidney Pratt had been unaware that he was fighting such an intruder, therefore escaping the same fate as Caleb.

Now he sat across from Ryan at a small table in one of the rooms. Ryan was smart and capable for his age and fully aware of what he possessed; Hadley felt sure that it could be done this time, successfully.

As soon as he had a fixed location on Susan, he would flee here, abandon this place, and end this wretched identity. He would leave the boy here, safely, and then he would find her. After all these years, he would find her. He couldn't allow any distractions now, especially from the sinister ship from which he was about to mutiny. Now, he was in charge. He turned his cell phone off, as well as the satellite phone and video monitors, the quick alternatives since cell usage became limited throughout this vast underground.

"Ryan, I want you to look directly at me and focus with your telepathic mind when I speak to you," he said.

Ryan's face was hard, insolent, but he complied.

"Where is Susan Logan, right at this moment? Can you hear her?"

Ryan continued to stare bitterly at him then lifted his head up, his eyes casting a fixed gaze, his clairaudient ear searching through the silence. No sounds came to him.

"I can't hear her; I'm not hearing anything, right now."

"Ryan, try to focus; this is important. I'm asking you to search with your telepathic mind and utilize your clairaudient ear to hear any sounds. Try to merge your abilities, make them one."

Hadley's voice was urgent, impatient.

"Try again, Ryan. What about the others, the team? Where are they?"

At this point, Ryan failed to budge at the slightest hint of intimidation or pressure, his stare now protesting in apathetic abandonment.

"I told you; I don't hear anything, right now."

Hadley fixed an intense gaze into Ryan's eyes. He pictured his own mind and the boy's mind co-existing together, his intuition merging with the boy's thoughts and mental images. He closed his eyes and saw the smaller brain, and then something quick like a camera flash showed him a mental picture of the underground itself, then the room where Ryan had been kept. Another flash changed the scene, and he saw the image of them both at the table where they sat.

The next instant flash brought with it a bright, magnificent light, a pure painful whiteness that made his eyes wince. Then an image of a young man filled his mind. He tried to open his eyes, to react, to shake himself from the telepathic reverie, but could not.

The young man with the greenest eyes he'd ever seen encapsulated the vision, his reddish-brown hair and blustering shoulders seemed menacing even from the distance of another world. The threatening upward glare of the deep, sage green eyes stared as though they were pointing at Hadley, who now wriggled in the chair, trying to wrestle himself away from the frozen hold.

That same intuition he'd often felt, especially today, told him that the young man was Ryan's father; he kept coming closer and closer with those eyes that never blinked and pupils that grew larger and larger, enough to swallow his mind. Hadley let out a cry of pain that roused him out of the telepathic trance that had subdued him.

He felt numbness all over, and he steadied himself not to fall out of the chair as sleeping muscles sought to awaken. The daze of a dizzying spell left him aware, but out of touch, and he glanced up to see Ryan's expression change to one of surprise and automatic concern.

The boy was staring at his face, and through the numbness that began to lessen, Hadley felt a hot, wet stream trickle down his nose and settle upon the edge of his upper lip. He touched it with his fingers then pulled them away—blood.

"No," he said, placing all of his weight upon the chair to slowly rise. The chair slightly slid from under him, nearly dropping him to the floor, but he balanced it and steadied himself upright. He wiped the blood from his nose with his sleeve and looked around, disoriented.

Ryan watched as Hadley slowly shuffled his feet in an uncertain direction, searching around, as though he was missing something.

"Mr. Hadley?" Ryan addressed him in question mode. The only response that Hadley gave was a brief exhale of fatigue, and then he murmured a name…*Susan.*

* * * *

The passenger in the maroon Sedan had tried several times to reach Hadley on his cell phone; he was not answering the calls. The mysterious passenger had no luck with the satellite phone either. One of them had to be answered at all times.

"Perhaps he's already vacated," the driver said in a lifeless monotone.

"Those were not his instructions," the passenger said. "Besides, he is unaware of what is taking place. We must leave immediately; we cannot save Hadley or the boy now, if they're still there."

The passenger retrieved a small gadget, much like a cell phone in appearance, from the opposite inner pocket of his black suit and touched a few buttons.

"The computer systems will initiate the explosive self destruction sequence." The eerie voice of the passenger was similar in tone to that of the driver, yet older. "In exactly thirty minutes, the entire compound will be annihilated to bits and pieces, whether Hadley and the boy are there or not. Hadley has finally become a weak link; we must cut our losses..."

* * * *

Hadley was pacing back and forth, lost in minor confusion that was just enough to make him lose time. He pulled his cell phone out, turned it back on, and fumbled trying to close the screen that showed two missed calls, not that it mattered anymore. He attempted to place a call but only stared at the screen in confusion, then looked around him, his eyes gazing agog into the distance. Who would he call?

Suzy Q.

The nickname he remembered well, but he didn't have her number. He knew that—the fog was making him forget. He looked over at the boy, whose concern was now tinged with growing fear, seeing the blood from his nose spotting the floor in droplets. Hadley looked down at it and remembered Caleb.

So, he was now the aggressor; how did this happen? He wished he would have died in an effort to get out of here, but he didn't. The money was fantastic; he had never wanted for anything. His every need, every whim, was served to him on a platter. There had also been the fear, the fear of returning home with the realization that he was not the same person anymore, one way or another. Their continuous threats to his family, and also to Susan, became overwhelming. His life would have been over if anything had happened to them because of him.

He looked back at Ryan. How could he have wanted the same thing for this innocent child, to suffer the same existence as he had? His ability was a curse, and no one knew better than he did, right now. The boy was too young to realize it yet.

"You must leave here, Ryan," he said. "You must go."

Chapter Seventeen

She missed nearly broad siding a parked car in her haste and insurmountable shock, a stupor so great that she felt herself trying to move her lips to say something, but some strange paralysis only allowed her to make minimal moans of distress during the failed attempts. Her mind became incapable of sustaining the slightest thought of anything other than what she'd just been told: Mark, Hadley, the same person—impossible. How could this be? She felt the bitter disappointment at not waking in her bed and discovering it all to be a nightmare.

She had stopped at Ed's Diner, only to be told that Wiley and the team had left minutes before. Susan turned and left without saying a word; she knew where they had gone, to the old mining section of town. Leah saw the vision in her office, and the girl described everything to perfection. If she didn't find them, she was going alone to hunt for Hadley; if Sidney was right, he would be holding Ryan in that old, renovated mining facility.

She would go there and prove that Sidney was wrong; he had to be, but then she thought back to the day when she first met Ryan, and she'd been reading his file in her office. When she read of the boy's abilities, she was overcome with the memories of Mark and how similar their psychic abilities were, more so than Sidney's.

Roman Hadley was suspected of belonging to the same psychic ilk.

Every time she held out hope that it wasn't true, that thought came back to her, draping a dark curtain over her pounding heart. Her attention to the road in front of her waned, and she drove on, oblivious to the rural scenes that passed her by, bringing her closer to her destination.

It had been over forty years, forty-two, to be exact, since she last saw Mark. The day that his number was called at the draft office rally was the day it had ended for them. They spent the next few days together before he'd left on the bus for boot camp. Those last moments were taking place in her mind all over again: the rush to leave, the promises of hope they'd exchanged, while unspoken premonitions of dread danced on their lips, the tears before he'd boarded the bus, and the way he'd squeezed her hard. She still recalled the familiar song that played on the car radio as she drove him to the station...

Nights in white satin, never reaching the end...
Letters I've written, never meaning to send.
Beauty I'd always missed with these eyes before.
Just what the truth is. I can't say anymore.
'Cos I love you... Yes, I love you. Oh how I love you.

The song played on in her mind, perfectly recorded, and she lived the moment over again with carbon copy clarity, as though that moment, and this moment in the car all these years later, were two connected points in time and space. Why did that song feel so damn relevant right now? Her heart felt as though the past forty-two years had never taken place.

Tears cascaded down her face, coaching the silent, sequestered sobs into a full, audible symphony. The unthinkable had consumed her, but through the windshield, she recognized the rural route winding out in front of her. She was so much closer to discovering the truth—once and for all.

* * * *

The old, desolate, rural valley that once served as a substantial mining district was home to only a handful of houses sparsely spread throughout. Lifeless, except for the few who lived there, the small territory could fit the definition of "ghost town" with its vast, vacated, and barren appearance, devoid of businesses, structures or vehicles. Street after street displayed defunct and abandoned remnants of old machinery that once roared and hissed.

Wiley pulled up alongside the old railroad tracks, his backup steadily but silently following behind. Ursula was pointing in a direction just north of where she, Leah, and Wiley sat in the car.

"There is an entranceway in that direction," she said. "It's hidden by some brush and foliage, but the entranceway leads to a tunnel, the tunnel leads to the compound."

"Okay, girls," Wiley said. "Now, I want you to stay calm, and stick with me at all times. You do and go what and when I tell you, understand?" They nodded. "I want us to quietly step out of the car so I can issue some last few instructions to my backup."

They exited the car as quietly and nonchalantly as did the small following procession that arrived behind them. Wiley had insisted that Brett bring his car because the group's van was out of the question; it would draw too much attention. The last thing Wiley wanted was for the inhabitants inside to become aware of the small cavalry outside. He walked over to them, instructing them to be waiting to get the girls away from the scene when the time came.

Wiley ordered his backup team to follow closely behind him and the girls, and after Ursula took them to the entranceway, they were to storm the tunnel. He supplied the blueprints to his team, unsure of any exit routes within the tunnel; Ursula hadn't noticed any, but Wiley stationed some of his team around the area, just in case.

He and the girls made it to the brush that covered a small, rectangular shaped, cave entrance that loomed a little over five feet in height, the team silently ready behind them. Once the brush was pulled away, Wiley could see that the width of the entrance was sizable, but the height was cramped, causing anyone over five feet, seven inches to duck when entering. He turned to them, and Ursula confirmed it as the entrance to the tunnel, while Leah identified it as the one in her vision.

"Walk about ten feet into the entrance," Ursula said, "turn right, and there is a tunnel. From there, after you walk about a hundred yards, an outside light will automatically turn on; it is initiated by movement." She had explained all of this to Wiley in the car, and now she repeated it as the FBI team listened intently.

"All right," Wiley said. "Team—remain on standby. I want you girls to go back to Brett's car, quickly but quietly."

The girls began to walk away as the team crouched into position, when a familiar Ford Taurus thundered into the location, leaving Brett's car in the dust that spun from its wheels. It kept coming closer, then noisily and carelessly pulled up over the old railroad tracks, bouncing its tires and banging its front end, landing with a smashing stop.

Susan Logan jumped out of her car and screamed...

"Wait! Wait!"

* * * *

The moment was a bittersweet one for Ryan, mixed with relief, joy, but concern as he watched the man now strangely stricken and bleeding from the nose. Hadley stumbled trying to get up then sat back down again, as though standing was too great an effort. Ryan couldn't be sure if it had been four or five days that he'd spent here, but it seemed like forever, and the man who had kidnapped him had just told him to leave.

Hadley turned his head back toward him.

"Go on," he said. "Did you hear me? I said, 'leave here.'" Ryan looked around, unsure of where to go, and when Hadley realized this, he pointed. "That way, down the corridor, keep walking until you see the double doors. Press the green button; they'll open. Then, go through the tunnel, Ryan...the tunnel."

The confusion on Hadley's face grew deeper, becoming an almost permanent fixture. He kept muttering about the tunnel, the tunnel that Ryan had never seen. He stood watching Hadley, and concern turned to alarm when a thicker stream of blood flowed from his nostril. He wanted out of here, but he had to get the man help.

The computers that were suddenly humming, buzzing, and uttering the sounds of oncoming malfunction quickly distracted Ryan's attention; something was happening. He looked at Hadley again; the man's color was fading.

He turned and ran in the direction Hadley had pointed to and didn't look back; he would find his way out, one way or another. His eyes searched around as he fled, not seeing the guards anywhere. Finally facing the double doors, he stood on his toes to press the green button, and as the doors opened wide, he could feel slight traces of cool, fresh air.

He followed which way the breeze touched him; it would obviously be the way to the tunnel. After walking for almost a minute, he saw the tunnel loom before him: dark, hollow, spooky. That's when he realized he was underground.

* * * *

Hadley was having sporadic moments of clarity; one moment he was confused as to what had happened, the other, he recalled letting the boy go, and he knew why. It was all over now; Ryan would find his way out of here. He couldn't waste time; he should have left with the boy, but he was confused.

The computers inside the compound were making the sounds of

haywire: buzzing, humming, bleeping so loudly when they had remained silent for so long. In one moment of clarity, he recalled just what that meant.

"In the event of a mandatory evacuation, the computers will initiate the self destruction sequence, destroying the compound and everything inside. You would have thirty minutes to clear out."

He remembered well the monotone voice. He didn't know how much time had passed, but he knew there wasn't much left, and he forced his weakened body to move faster. He had to find Susan now, before it was too late...

* * * *

"Wait!"

She screamed loud enough that her voice echoed through open space. Wiley ran to her, shushing her and grabbing hold of her shoulders to steady her. She was wild, trying to get her point out as Wiley tried to stifle her screams before she blew the entire operation. Dylan and Brett came running from the car, as did a few backup officers from their posts.

She broke down in tears, trying to force the words through her broken speech. Wiley held her as she cried on his shoulder.

"Susan, listen to me," he said. "I need you to calm down, and tell me what's wrong—*quietly*. You're loud enough that someone inside may hear you. If anyone finds out we're here…"

"Sidney says that Roman Hadley is Mark...*my Mark!*" She stepped back from him.

Dylan and Brett looked at each other and moved forward.

"Mark?" Wiley asked. "Who is Mark? Guys, what is she talking about?"

Dylan and Brett stood at either side of her, supporting her.

"Sidney said he knows Roman Hadley's real identity," she said, through her shaking, creaking voice. Her emotional collapse caused her legs to give way from under her, and Dylan caught her, then held her closely and tightly to smother her repetitive sobs. Suddenly, Dr. Susan Logan, the pillar of rational, sound, but relaxed and open thinking, was a quivering jellyfish of nerves caught in Dylan's arms.

Brett pulled Wiley away and explained to him that Mark was Susan's fiancé, presumed dead in the Vietnam War, and that Sidney had heard him many years ago.

"That doesn't make any sense," Wiley said, and as he thought for a moment, Susan broke away from Dylan and ran over to him, having overheard his misunderstanding.

"I never told Sidney that Mark was a clairaudient. He identified Mark's voice as being the same as Hadley's. He never put the two together until now. Mark disappeared from Vietnam; we never heard another word from him, outside of his last few letters." She sounded more composed, just anxious to make him understand what she was saying.

"What year did Mark go missing?" Wiley's curiosity peaked.

"1970," she said."

"That was right around the time of the defections from the FBI's psychic research testing." Hadley spoke this verbal thought more to himself than to anyone else.

"If Roman Hadley is your Mark, then he must have been recruited by this group right out of Vietnam. So, you mean to tell me that he has gone all of these years without contacting anyone: you, his family, and friends?"

"I only know what Sidney told me," she said. "I am going to prove that it isn't true." Her voice cracked on her last words, and instantly, they were quieting her.

"You have to let me go in there," she said, and then her words were cut short.

"Agent Wiley?" One of the backup officers perched at the entranceway called out. "Someone is coming out!"

The officers backed away from the cave-like entry, poised into position and aiming their weapons.

Ryan walked out of the entranceway.

Rifles were lowered at the surprise, and gasps were heard in unison. Several officers ran to him, scooping him up with quick-moving arms and examining him to see if he was hurt. They then turned him over to Wiley and the team of investigators.

Chapter Eighteen

They crowded around Ryan, hugging him, fussing, and lifting him in the air. Ursula was one of the first to grab him in a hold, rejoicing that he was safe.

"Thank you," he said to her.

"No need to thank me," she said. "I told you I'd get you out of there."

"Okay, get back!" Wiley ordered. "Everyone get back as far as possible."

"I'm going in with you!" Susan said, as she realized they were about to go in. She was almost angered, forceful in her persuasion, grabbing the sleeve of his jacket and holding on.

"All right," he said. "That's not a bad idea, you may be of some help, especially if it is him, but they need to go in first, incase he's armed."

"He wouldn't—"

"It doesn't matter. I can't risk anyone else's life, not yours, not theirs."

"Tell them not to shoot," she pleaded. "Please tell them—"

"They only would if he's armed. Now, that may not be the case. That's why we would need you, but Susan, you need to be in control of yourself, understand?"

She closed her eyes, took a deep breath, and nodded her head.

"Let's go!" Wiley called out softly, and the armed backup team rushed the entranceway, moving in the direction that Ryan and Ursula had detailed, as the game plan had slightly changed. Wiley had a protective arm around Susan as they followed. The others stayed behind, gathered around the vehicles, guarded by the remaining backup team.

A fraction of the raiding agents scattered in different directions, searching to find the guards that Ryan claimed had disappeared. As they moved aside, Wiley, Susan, and the escorting agents, moved faster through the underground, the double doors, and into the compound.

The dankness of earth greeted their nostrils, while the runaway sounds of existing, but malfunctioning technology greeted their ears. The compound was fully constructed as a medical research facility and was suited with all the accommodations: sterile rooms, bunkers, and computers that now signaled the sounds of overwhelming alarm. They winced at the high-pitched beeping, gurgling, and humming that seemed to grow louder as if each repetitive sound was an ascending alert.

Then, one of the team leaders in front shouted over the noise.

"Move back, move back!"

The officers stepped aside, and through the space that was made, they saw a man, huddling and struggling to gain foot on the ground. Wiley noticed the small, dark red pools on the floor beneath the man.

"Wait!" Wiley shouted. "He's unarmed, possibly injured!"

Hadley was trying to balance himself against one of the rails that lined the length across the compound walls, fighting a fading equilibrium. The blood now stained his shirt and trailed in the small pools behind him as he staggered. His eyes were lost, glossy, serene.

* * * *

He looked up and over at the faces that stared at him, the weapons still cautiously pointed at him, then the face he'd known and loved so well appeared, coming closer to him out of a vortex of lost time. He'd seen her picture in a psychological journal, once, throughout the lost years, her web page a few times, but now as she came closer, inspecting his every feature, he realized it was the first time he'd really seen her face since that day at the bus station in 1969.

His heart dropped at the sight of her, and she knew it. Tears formed and streaked her face at some instant recognition. Time had not touched her beautiful face, and the quick feeling of pride interrupted his agony, if only for a moment. There she was in front of him, her presence almost cancelling out the last four decades, as though they had never occurred. Though now he reasoned it was too late, enduring what he felt were the last moments of his life, feeling them slowly slipping away...

* * * *

She saw the man hanging onto the rail, but it was hard to see his face at first. As the officers stepped aside, she took a few steps closer, and Wiley didn't stop her. *Is it him?* She was cautious, skeptical. Whoever it was needed medical attention because that dark substance that surrounded him and stained his attire was definitely blood.

The hair, it was similar, now with gray streaks touching the temples and shading the sheen darkness. She kept studying the face as she moved closer to him. He stared at her sideways, as though he'd been expecting her, and the eyes that she'd gazed into throughout her youth stared back at her. A sword pierced her heart from top to bottom, and the pain it created caused her face to twist at the bittersweet reality...

He was alive! She ran to him, grabbing both sides of his face in her hands, searching his eyes to be sure. Their hearts cried out in perfect synchronicity, bearing tears of recognition and wringing endless, lamenting sounds of sorrow from their voices.

"Mark!" She screamed as she clutched him to her, his blood now staining her hands and clothes. "Mark? Why?" She pulled away and looked into his face one more time. The tears welled in his eyes.

"Suzy Q," he said, recalling his pet name for her.

"My God, what happened to you? Where have you been? *Why?*"

Her voice grew louder as the questions wore thin; what else was there to ask?

"We have to get you to the hospital," she said, her voice now rushing. She turned to Wiley, who was now radioing for an ambulance. "Oh, God!" She screamed as the blood that streaked his face from his nose now seemed to be everywhere. His nose, just like Sidney, she thought. Cerebral hemorrhage...

"There isn't much time," he said. "You have to leave me here, Susan."

He struggled to speak, but her protests overpowered his weakened attempts. She could hear Wiley giving directions to the compound. She laid his head back and applied pressure to the side of his nose. Then she softly stroked his forehead.

"The boy?" he asked.

"Ryan is safe outside."

"Not safe," he said, struggling. "Got to get away from here..."

She tried to hush him, until he started pointing, his finger targeting the direction of the computers. She turned and looked at the machines that continued to squeal. Wiley finished the emergency call then squatted down beside them.

"Too late," the former Roman Hadley said, still pointing. "Go, get out!"

Wiley turned his head toward the rampaging machines as he remembered the underground compound in Washington—nothing left but bits and pieces. His eyes grew wide at the realization that Hadley was right; it was too late...

* * * *

The team, along with Ursula, stood outside by the vehicles discussing the events of the last few days. Ryan was detailing how the last thing he remembered in the men's room was someone grabbing him from behind and how he could smell almonds.

"Chloroform," Brett said. "That's why we didn't hear anything." Just the thought of it caused them all to look at each other, realizing what Ryan may have been too young to understand. Ursula explained her role in the situation exactly as she had to Wiley, and Ryan backed her up.

"You really should be commended, Ursula," Dylan said. "We may not have found him in time if it weren't for you. Hadley could have taken him anywhere."

Ursula lowered her eyes, humbled.

"Well, lucky for you that I'm pretty unlucky, right?" Ursula joked with Ryan, embracing her pal and patting his back.

They hadn't noticed Leah Leeds as she stepped away and moved in a fixed trance toward the entranceway...

* * * *

Something was happening; she was seeing Ian again. He motioned her away from the small gathering by the vehicles, and she followed him to the entrance. He was pointing at it. He looked back at her then looked again at the entrance.

She gazed past the cavernous entrance with her third eye, and letting it take over, she saw the tunnel, spiral after spiral, straight to a set of sliding doors, a blinking green light above them, white rooms, darkened corridors. Then she saw Susan on the floor, holding someone, Hadley, Wiley using the handheld radio, blood, the computers, lights, blinking, flashing; then there was nothing but a huge fireball, debris being flung miles into the air.

The visions stopped just as Dylan called to her...

"Leah, where are you going? What's wrong?"

The chilled October air struck her face, awakening her. She realized the here and now as Ian was gone with the flashing visions. She turned herself around slowly from the shock of what she'd just seen, and then she screamed...

"It's gonna blow! Move! It's gonna blow!"

* * * *

The scene of the underground compound in Washington had flashed through his mind with its collapsed walls imprisoning piles of scattered debris underneath, a result of a mass explosion. The Bureau had always assumed that the destruction was deliberately set by the group, some type of manually instituted bomb. But as he looked now at the computers with their blinking screens and screeching sounds of alert, he realized why that was happening, and it was a harsh dawn that enlightened him.

The computers were initiating an explosive, self-destruction sequence; the entire compound was about to be destroyed.

"Listen up!" Wiley shouted. "This place is about to explode! I need all but two of you to move out! Two of you will help get him out of here! *MOVE, NOW!*"

The thundering shuffling of feet rumbled across the floor, and the remaining officers attempted to grab a secure hold of the man on the floor, when Susan began screaming. Blood was gushing everywhere now. The color in the man's face was draining away, and the curtain call of Roman Hadley was leaving a once, young soldier to die on a cold floor beneath the earth.

He stared at her through glossy, dying eyes and whispered...

"Susan...Suzy Q...I have always...loved you...never stopped..."

He gasped and swallowed, fighting the final breath, and his eyes continued to stare at her. She screamed his name once more in a loud, final plea, and the sound of the soldier's name echoed through the underground.

Her grief instantly set by the final gasp that escaped him.

"No! No!" Wiley grabbed her and tried to pull her up, but she fought him.

"There's nothing you can do, Susan; he's gone!" He repeated those last two words, shaking her into acceptance as the sounds of oncoming fate loudly prophesied approaching doom. The beeping became louder, faster, like the preamble of a rocket launch.

"Move, now!" At Wiley's command, the two assisting officers

turned, ran, and disappeared. The sounds were getting faster as a mixture of earth and plaster began to lightly shower from above.

"Susan! We've got to get out, now!"

She continued to fight him, unwilling to leave the man, whom to her was still somehow alive. Not allowing her insanity to take over, he scooped her up in his arms and ran the same way they had come.

* * * *

Leah ran with her arms flailing at the team and the remaining officers.

"Get back!" She screamed. *"It's gonna blow!"*

The team didn't question her, running as fast and as far from the compound as possible. The remaining officers took cover in a somewhat skeptical fashion until their fellow officers stormed out of the entrance, shouting orders to move out.

Susan, Leah thought. Where was she?

The team was huddled, with Ryan, approximately a hundred yards away from the entrance. They watched and waited...

* * * *

He had made it, carrying her, through the double doors and into the tunnel. It would be faster this way, if they made it at all. She remained in a state of stubborn immobility, and it was either carry her, or drag her, and there hadn't been time to decide.

The tunnel was much harder to move through than the compound. He crouched and ran as best as he could, knowing her screams of Mark's name would be the last things he heard if he didn't move faster. The sweat poured down his face, drenching him, flowing into his eyes and clouding his vision.

He could feel a rumbling beneath his feet, and instinct caused him to turn his head slightly to inspect the distance behind him. From the corner of his eye, he saw a bright flash of white ignite and spread from depths below, and the sound of the initial blast seemed almost far away, though it started to rain down debris on their heads. The entranceway was only feet ahead, but a scurrying inferno blistered fast behind him. His legs moved faster when he felt the growing heat touch his back.

* * * *

Leah watched the entranceway from afar and prayed.

"Oh, God," she said. "What are we going to tell Sidney, if she doesn't make it out?" The tone of her voice was tortured by continuous fear and tragedy. The looks on the rest of their faces didn't console her, as they looked away or intently at her with fear and despair, preparing for the inevitable.

They heard a rumbling noise as the ground quaked beneath their feet. It was no earthquake, not here. Off in the distance to the right of where they assembled, a bright flash of white and orange erupted from the ground, the rumbling sound segueing into the splitting, cracking clamor of explosion.

But as quickly as they cowered, they jumped to their feet, and several officers ran toward the entrance as two figures emerged from it.

They watched as Wiley bolted from the entrance, clutching Susan in his arms. Then the ground convulsed beneath them all, and they swayed back and forth trying to maintain balance. The roar of the blast ripped around them, loud, threatening, traumatically magnifying the fear of death. Leah watched as the orange fireball now reached for the sky, flinging debris high into the air to rain down upon them, just as her third eye had shown her.

Bits of stone, wood, and metal were falling from the sky, along with the floating flickers of flame that danced with the cold wind. Though the blast had knocked them to the ground, Wiley and Susan made it safely away with only mere seconds sparing their lives. The officers ran over to them, helping them away from the collapsed entrance.

Susan's frenzied hysteria was somewhat softened by the shock of the blast into desperate moans and mourning wails that led to heaving breaths of hyperventilation. They sat her down on the hood of Brett's car, and Leah held her closely as the rest gathered around her.

"It's going to be all right, now, Susan," Leah said. "You'll see." She rocked her back and forth. "Come back to us; we need you."

In the distance, the sounds of approaching ambulance sirens combined with the whines of fire engines, brazenly blaring out through the vast, quiet district that had otherwise remained silent.

They strapped Susan to a gurney when they arrived, the shock causing her body to tremble in trauma. Leah held her hand, finding herself riding in yet another ambulance.

"She'll be all right," the EMT said. "Shock—it'll wear off." They began to fuss over Wiley, who kept insisting that he was fine, but standard procedure prevailed. He was examined and deemed uninjured.

"I want you to take the boy; he needs to be looked at," Wiley said, and walked over to Ryan. "Everything is going to be okay, Ryan. I'm going to call your mother, and she will meet us at the hospital. If everything checks out, you can go home."

The color was already returning to Ryan's face, flushing away the paleness from his brief stint underground, and Wiley's words struck relief in the hearts of the investigators; it had been a long week...

Chapter Nineteen

At the hospital, Annie Quinn had been waiting for her son, and when the investigators walked through the ER doors with him, he ran into her open arms. She remained with him as he was examined and pronounced healthy and unharmed. Ryan was free to return home and resume his life.

She thanked Agent Wiley for finding her son.

"I appreciate that," he said. "But mainly, you have these two ladies to thank for getting Ryan back so quickly." Wiley explained to her the role that Ursula played and how Leah's vision had come to her.

"How do I ever thank you?" she said to Ursula. "Thank you for saving him, for risking your life."

Ursula assured her that she only did what anyone else would have. Annie then turned to Leah.

"You, I am forever in your debt," she said, "both of you." Like Ursula, Leah downplayed her actions, and then answered the question Annie stuttered in asking. Wiley had told her of Leah's vision.

"Yes, it was him," Leah said, before she could finish. "Ryan's father saved him tonight."

Annie lowered her head, stunned and saddened by the slightest tinge of regret.

Susan was treated for shock, sedated, and admitted overnight. Leah and the rest of the team had left her sleeping soundly in the hospital room. They made one last stop before calling it a day, and that was to see Sidney...

* * * *

Ryan ran into the room and hugged him gently. Sidney was thrilled to see him and equally surprised to see the joy in Annie's face.

"I'm so glad you're here, Ryan," he said. "I thank God they found you, and I am so sorry that you got mixed up in all of this."

"No, Sidney. It was me who called out to you; I wanted to help."

Just then, Annie broke in.

"Yeah, and if he wouldn't have snuck out on me, he wouldn't have ended up where he did, now would he?" She said this to her son, and then turned her attention to Sidney.

"I want you to know, all of you," she said, looking around, "that I don't blame any of you for this. I understand a lot more now than I ever did. I also realize that I am partially responsible for this, if I hadn't ignored my son—"

"Don't," Sidney said. "You were faced with something that is very hard to understand, that is frightening to most people, and extremely difficult to comprehend. I don't blame my parents for their response to my ability; I just thought they loved me more than their fear. But everyone can see, Annie, that you love your son very much."

"Yes," Leah said. "You suffered Hell in your own life because of someone who abused their ability, used it in ways to harm. I understand that about you now."

Leah touched Annie's shoulder then said softly,

"And in the end, he redeemed himself."

The wide-eyed wonder in Annie's eyes met the look of unsurprised experience in the eyes of the seer.

"Well, I say we all go home and get some much needed rest," Dylan said. "Because there is one more thing: Wiley wants to meet with us all in a few days, as soon as Susan is able to be here. He says there are unanswered questions that he hopes to be able to answer by then."

"Well, I'm not going anywhere," Sidney said, pointing to the various monitors that surrounded him and sounding more like himself every minute.

Then sleepy heads stirred, while yawns of exhaustion began to spread in contagion. They exchanged their nightly goodbyes and turned to leave, when Dylan spoke up again.

"Oh, yeah, by the way, Sid, we may have another investigator on our hands."

"Really?" Sidney said, lifting his head, his distraction interrupted.

"Yeah, she's the listener who helped us find Ryan. I think you're going to like her; she's amazing. Her name is Ursula."

Dylan's teasing of the truth ignited small smirks of laughter from the team.

"Oh, I see," Sidney said. "Replaced me already, huh? Fine, get out. What the hell kind of a name is Ursula anyway?"

The laughter became louder out in the corridor.

* * * *

Sidney sat back in bed, impressed that his sense of humor had returned after everything. Now as the room was silent and the outside dusk turned into night, the seriousness set in with it. He sat and thought about how Hadley had been conning them the whole time, stalking him over his ability, then turning to Ryan, an innocent child.

He realized that when he'd heard Mark's voice as a boy, he'd been tracking him not only over his ability, but as a connection to Susan. He had been following her all these years, through him. He felt slightly angered at the time wasted not recognizing that Hadley's voice and Mark's were one and the same. He felt as though he had failed Susan; he was devastated by her broken heart.

But then he thought of Tracy Kimball, and how she'd brought it all together for him, inducing him to remember the voices. He'd always known that there was life after death, but now he'd seen it. His heart would always be grateful toward her, and he felt the presence of a friend watching over him.

Chapter Twenty

Another three days had passed since Ryan was found, three days since the truth about Hadley, not to mention the explosion, had left Susan in a state of shock. Now, Sidney became anxious to leave the hospital; he could recover just as well in bed at home. Dr. Talbot had taken it as a good sign; Sidney was even up and walking for a brief period every day. But today, he ordered that Sidney be brought to Wiley's meeting in a wheelchair.

Sidney dreaded having to listen to the details of what Wiley had uncovered regarding Hadley, or Mark, that is. He worried about how much more of the details Susan could bear. How much more could her already broken heart endure? She had been released yesterday, and Sidney was allowed to see her beforehand, with his nurse and a wheelchair, of course. It was the first time he'd seen her since the explosion.

She appeared forlorn, distracted by some vivid world of past memories that kept her prisoner. Her eyes were lifeless, devoid of that spark that made her Susan.

"Hello, Sidney," she said to him in a flat, even tone. "How are you?"

"Not *me*," he said. "How are *you*?"

She shrugged.

"You were right, Sidney. It was him, and all these years I'd wondered..." Her words were slow, dramatically drawn, her eyes squinting and gazing indirectly, remembering the years. She shook her head and looked at him.

"I'll be all right, Sidney, just going to take some getting over. I still don't believe it," she said, now looking him straight in the eyes.

"I know," he said. "But we are all here for you, Susan, especially me."

Now, he was being wheeled to the meeting in the lounge where it had all begun. Wiley felt that it was more suitable than squeezing everyone into Sidney's room. Susan would be there, as well as the team, Ryan and Annie, and this young woman that he kept hearing about, who helped find Ryan.

His nurse propped the lounge door open and wheeled him inside. Everyone's faces met his, as though he were the awaited guest, yet he wasn't. Susan was there, looking a little better than the day before, but expressionless, saddened. Dylan, Brett, Leah, and Annie were standing alongside a short young woman with dark hair and beautiful eyes.

"Sidney, this is Ursula," Dylan said, introducing her. She stepped forward and extended her hand, offering a handshake.

Sidney reached from the chair and shook her hand.

"Ursula, this is Sidney Pratt," Dylan concluded.

"Ursula, what a beautiful name," Sidney said, as Dylan cleared his throat, and Brett and Leah hung their heads, biting their lips.

"Thank you," she said. "It's so nice to meet you, Sidney."

"Thank you, Ursula, for all you've done for Ryan and for us. You're a real hero or heroine..." She laughed at his flattery. "So, I hear you're quite the clairaudient?"

"Yes, well, I've heard the same of you," she said.

"Yeah, well, let's compare notes sometime soon." Sidney's voice no longer threatened to provoke laughter from his colleagues.

"I'd love to," she said.

Ryan hugged Sidney when he saw him, and they all exchanged greetings, then changed the subject, while they waited for Wiley to arrive.

* * * *

Wiley rode in the elevator on his way to the lounge. He dreaded this meeting only because of Susan Logan, but this mystery was about to be revealed once and for all, and the sooner the better. Susan was about to discover everything that had happened to Mark, and it was all because of the envelope he held in his hand.

Since the explosion, the Bureau had obtained something they were never in possession of before, during the investigation of Roman Hadley: his true identity. Once they began to investigate the name Mark Banner, the mystery of Roman Hadley had unfolded. The group had worked wonders in eradicating his true identity, but Mark had left something behind, something they hadn't noticed.

He hadn't kept a journal; that would have been too risky. But he did manage to document his entire story, leaving it behind in a twenty page letter addressed to Susan Logan. It had been uncovered in a safety deposit box in a bank in Pittsburgh, and now Wiley would deliver it to Susan, though not before explaining the story to everyone. He stuck the letter back in his inner jacket pocket; he would hand it to her after he spoke, deciding it was more appropriate.

Perspiration gathered on his forehead at the given task.

Tensions seemed to both ease and stir as he opened the door to the lounge and entered; expectant faces stared back at him in anticipation. He asked everyone to be seated so that he could begin.

The younger members of the group sat around the table, except Leah, who took a seat next to Susan on the couch.

"Let me start by saying that you all know how and why we became involved in what occurred this past week, and why we're here. A man most of you knew as a university benefactor and head coordinator of the Paranormal Research and Investigative Society kidnapped a young boy. The man you knew of as Roman Hadley was an imposter.

"Hadley was using the society as a cover for his real involvement with a rogue group of psychics, once part of the FBI's remote psychic studies until they disappeared into thin air, having evaded us for many years. They'd been conducting remote viewing and listening studies on their own and committing various acts of espionage, all through the use of psychic abilities."

This is the part that made him squeamish. He looked at Susan, as though cuing her to be ready.

"Hadley's real identity was that of Mark Steven Banner, a former associate of our friend, Dr. Logan." Wiley regretted using the formality of associate; he never meant to minimize who Mark was to her. Normally, he wouldn't have given it a second thought, but he'd become fond of Susan Logan.

"We now have reason to believe that Hadley, or should I say, Mark's involvement was not entirely voluntary. We've discovered falsified documents stating that Mark Banner was classified MIA during Vietnam. In fact, he had never been a POW. The group had abducted him from Vietnam, after an incident took place over there that roused attention to his psychic ability, an ability of which, Dr. Logan, I assume you were aware?"

His tone was rational and appeasing when he asked her. She cast her eyes downward then stood and walked to the coffee bar, her back turned.

"I'd assumed he'd died; I never saw any need to mention that he was a clairaudient. When Sidney first heard Mark, I wanted to know more, but I didn't tell him why. Sidney had assumed Mark was dead because as a child, he only knew he was capable of hearing the dead speak to him." A brief pause filled the room as she stirred her coffee. "We were going to be married, but he never came home." Her voice sounded lost, and when another appropriate pause had passed, Wiley continued.

"Eventually, the group threatened him and his loved ones, forcing him to remain, to live out his life toward their goals and the exploration of who he was psychically. They even resorted to blackmail, framing him as an accomplice, much as he'd almost done to Ursula, even threatening to twist the story of how he got there and threatening him with court marshal.

"The group had assigned him a new identity, that of Roman Hadley, an FBI agent; the cover would pass for many years under our noses. The years of his compliance were luxuriously compensated with whatever he wanted; however, it didn't compensate for the life that was stolen from him, nor the love that was stolen from him."

He spoke those words in Susan's direction. She was listening while her eyes were gazing at the opposite wall; she'd been transfixed in thought ever since he mentioned Mark's loved ones being threatened.

"He searched for a way out, but the hierarchy of authority within this group changed hands over the years, constantly monitoring his every move, probing his thoughts with their own telepathic minds, clairaudient ears, and watchful eyes. He became virtually a psychic prisoner.

"Through the years, Hadley's clairaudient and telepathic abilities had waned. He was not as useful in his latter age to the group as he once was. After studying Sidney Pratt for many years, a new possibility presented itself to Hadley and the group."

"Ryan," Sidney interjected.

"Yes," Wiley said. "With the discovery of Ryan, the group found someone that could possibly take them to heights never reached before, and Hadley also got a way out, that is, if they would have let him go. You see, they needed Hadley to run things; we're sure of that. But what we're unable to understand is why these people could not be a visible factor in their operation. It was so clandestine that Hadley himself mimicked the anonymity with the paranormal society. Why couldn't these people be seen?

"Hadley was eventually torn between bargaining, that is, trading himself for Ryan, or mutinying, disappearing, and leaving Ryan behind to be discovered. The growing amount of pressure he was under was insurmountable, possibly edging him toward a breakdown."

"Well, wait a minute," Sidney said. "How do you know all of this?" The other investigators looked at Wiley with the same curiosity. He pulled the envelope from his pocket.

"Hadley had left behind a long letter for Dr. Logan," he said, watching her turn her face sideways to him. "He explains everything from the very beginning into today. I am sorry that we had to intercept the letter, Susan, but it is evidence in an investigation. At this point, the original copy now belongs to you."

He handed it to her, and she simply stared at her name on the opened envelope written in Mark's handwriting. Wiley could see that she didn't have the courage to read it now; she would save it for later.

"Susan," Wiley said. "There is more to the blackmail than just the frame-up job. I think if I reveal it now, it would be better for you to hear it that way. It's your call."

"Go ahead," she said, taking a deep breath and sitting back down.

"They played a Catch-22 game with Mark, enticing him to cooperate with false promises of returning home. One of his captors at the time was a former agent, once part of the group that broke away from the Bureau's studies; his name was Foster. Foster accused Mark of killing his accomplice, Caleb West, a remote viewer also once with the FBI program.

"Mark had discovered a hidden unique ability known as telepathic intrusion, and when he focused it on Caleb, it resulted in his death from a cerebral hemorrhage. Foster decided to eliminate Mark, whom he now considered to be a liability or loose cannon.

"When Foster tried to kill Mark, Mark responded as a soldier and defended himself, or at least, what he describes in the letter is self defense. Mark killed Foster, as well as another accomplice, a woman named Myra. And so the blackmail continued for years."

"I've come to a conclusion on my own, Agent Wiley," Sidney spoke up. "I think Hadley, not understanding this thing called telepathic intrusion, caused my own episode. We know now that he was listening to us, remotely, the night of Tracy Kimball's accident; my headaches began shortly after that."

"Sidney, he would never have intended—" Susan said.

"I know," Sidney said. "But isn't it ironic that he died the same way as Caleb?"

"He'd been trying to get inside *my* mind," Ryan said, nervously. "As he was trying to read my thoughts, something happened to him; the blood just started flowing from his nose, like something stopped him."

Silence filled the room as they all looked at the boy, realizing that the strange inheritance had been passed on, and that what went around had come back around.

"I wonder what it was," he said.

"I have a very good idea what, or who, it was," Leah said. No one said another word.

* * * *

After the meeting was over, Wiley bid his goodbyes to everyone, and Annie thanked him one last time for finding her son.

"You stay safe, Ryan." he said. "Don't let this bring you down. Keep up your work with the team and Dr. Logan. They will help you through this."

"He will," Annie said. "I'll make sure this time."

The three of them left the hospital, and as Annie and Ryan drove home, the boy broke the awkward silence that seemed to be setting in everywhere.

"Mom, you know what I think? I think Dad somehow saved me. I wasn't hearing him for awhile, but I think he was there."

Annie smiled at how smart her son was.

"I think so too, Ryan. I really do."

* * * *

Susan and the rest of the team, including Ursula, gathered in Sidney's room. Dr. Talbot had just given Sidney the news that he could be released the next day, so long as he abided by the doctor's orders of complete bed rest, no stress, and to keep all of his ensuing medical appointments.

The team assured him that they would look after Sidney, and Talbot left the room. Then, they motioned for Dylan to make the respective announcements.

"Susan," he said. "I have heard word from the society's sponsors, as of today. They, along with the rest of us, are unanimous in concluding that we would like you to assume the position of the society's coordinator. We feel that you are the best choice to lead our efforts."

Susan looked at them.

"You mean, replace Roman Hadley?"

"That's right," Dylan said.

"I accept." Her answer was quick, assertive.

"Also, I'd like to congratulate Ursula," Dylan said. "We have asked her to come and work and explore with us, and she has agreed."

A light applause was directed at her.

"Thank you," she said. "Though I'm sure between my studies and work, my attendance will be sporadic, but I am thrilled and excited."

"We are happy to have you," Dylan said.

"That's right," Sidney said. "And now that I'll be going home, maybe you can come over with the rest of the team and fill us in on your story?"

She agreed, and Susan noticed as three kids parading in costume for the patients entered Sidney's room and called in a not-so-loud voice...

"Trick-or-Treat!"

"Halloween, already," Susan said. "I'm so glad that we can call an end to this horrible month once and for all."

And all agreed.

Epilogue

Leah was grateful, relieved to be back in the plush comfort of her own bed. Recently, the days seemed unending, and tonight she was sure to sleep soundlessly, or so she thought.

She couldn't actually recall falling asleep, as the day's events seemed to merge with the past, as she lay immobile. But in the dream state, it all played out for her again...

She'd been in Cedar Manor; it was just as she remembered, as though time had never passed. She was chasing the runaway spool of yarn that unwound down the hallway, running after it as it moved on its own to some predestined location. Then, she saw Agnes in the rocker; they smiled at each other.

She jumped, ran, and played, reliving the playful joy of childhood. Suddenly the lights flickered on and off, and she heard the sound of her father's voice calling out to her...

"Leah, where are you?"

Her mother's voice came next...

"Leah! Stay away from that mirror!"

In the dream, she could see and hear the ticking of the grandfather clock...

Tick, tock, tick, tock,

The swaying of its second hand back and forth was interrupted by flashing visions: the basement, then the clock, the face of the dead woman murdered by Agnes' son, the clock, her mother's feet swaying beneath her skirt as her body hung from the swaying noose tied to the balcony, the clock, silence except for the ticking. Then, she heard the breathing again, and the rapid, grating, respiration grew louder, causing the frightened little girl to run as she heard it nearing.

She ran down the hallway, faster and faster, closer and closer toward the mirror. She wasn't allowed to go near it, but something was drawing her there. She was amazed at how quickly she covered more ground than usual. The breath heaved faster and harder as the little girl now faced the mirror and looked inside. There wasn't anything there...

Then it leapt out at her. The ghastly, Hellish reflection had been hiding off to the side, somewhere inside the mirror. Its misshapen face was deformed, decayed from what looked like death and decomposition. The hair was a long rotten mane, lifeless like straw. The breathing was coming from it, and it was staring at her with a cold, dead, discolored eye, as though it meant to find her. The breath became faster. It knew her; it had found her, and it was waiting for her, its breath heaving loudly.

She shot up from the bed, shedding sleep, her heart beating wildly in her chest, and the sound of the breathing now belonged to her. The sweat poured down her face, and she felt it soak her nightshirt. She switched on the light as quickly as possible.

Reality didn't seem to bring the same relief that it normally did; the nightmare was vivid, fresh, the details etching into her mind. She couldn't live this way anymore, and realized in the bright waking light of her bedroom what must be done. It was time to confront it. One way or another, it was time to go back into that house...

CITATIONS

The Moody Blues, "Nights In White Satin" from <u>Days of Future Passed.</u> Justin Hayward. Prod: Tony Clarke. Derham Records.

Christopher Carrolli

www.ingramcontent.com/pod-product-compliance
Lightning Source LLC
Chambersburg PA
CBHW020440180626
46812CB00003B/1330